W9-DJQ-208

DISCARDED

SCARED TO DEATH

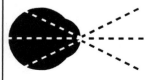

This Large Print Book carries the
Seal of Approval of N.A.V.H.

SCARED TO DEATH

DEBBY GIUSTI

THORNDIKE PRESS
A part of Gale, Cengage Learning

GALE
CENGAGE Learning

Detroit • New York • San Francisco • New Haven, Conn • Waterville, Maine • London

GALE
CENGAGE Learning

Thorndike Press® Large Print Christian Fiction.
The text of this Large Print edition is unabridged.
Other aspects of the book may vary from the original edition.
Set in 16 pt. Plantin.
Printed on permanent paper.

LIBRARY OF CONGRESS CATALOGING-IN-PUBLICATION DATA

Giusti, Debby.
  Scared to death / by Debby Giusti.
    p. cm. — (Thorndike Press large print Christian fiction)
    ISBN-13: 978-1-4104-0487-9 (hardcover : alk. paper)
    ISBN-10: 1-4104-0487-0 (hardcover : alk. paper)
    1. Women scientists — Fiction. 2. Georgia — Fiction. 3. Large type books. I. Title.
  PS3607.I73S33 2008
  813'.6—dc22   2007044716

Published in 2008 by arrangement with Harlequin Books S.A.

Printed in the United States of America
1 2 3 4 5 6 7 12 11 10 09 08

I love the Lord, for he heard my voice;
He heard my cry for mercy.
— *Psalms* 116:1

To Tony
My husband, my hero

To Elizabeth, Joseph and Mary
I am so proud of each of you

To Darlene Buchholz, Annie Oortman,
Dianna Love Snell and Sharon Yanish
Good friends and
great critique partners

To Krista Stroever
For your suggestions and guidance

To Jessica Alvarez
For your help throughout
the editing process

ONE

"Kate. I need your help."

The urgency in the caller's voice made Kate Murphy's heart race. "Who . . . Who is this?"

"It's Tina."

Kate flinched at the name she hadn't heard in three years. Images of death and betrayal flashed through her mind. Images Kate wanted to forget.

"Maybe I shouldn't have called." Tina's words were clipped, her tone wary. "It's been so long, but —"

Cupping a free hand over her ear, Kate tried to drown out the whirr of the centrifuges that filled the medical research lab where she worked.

"Wait, let me step into the hallway. I'll be able to hear better." Static crackled across the line as Kate changed locations. "Still there?"

"I know this sounds crazy, but I stumbled

across something in the woods and need your medical expertise. Remember when you used to joke about what would happen if the bad guys ever unlocked the secrets of science?"

"Yeah?"

"I think they have."

The tone of Tina's voice made Kate's skin crawl.

Her former friend was right. The whole thing *did* sound crazy. "How'd you find me, Tina?"

"Your name was in the paper. The article said you worked at Bannister Scientific in Atlanta."

Kate raked a hand through her hair. She had only given one interview and suddenly she was front-page news. "I can't leave. I'm in the middle of a project."

No reason to mention her research had been put on hold. Tomorrow started her two-week probation while Bannister Scientific decided whether she'd keep her job.

"It's Friday," Tina pleaded. "Surely you get the weekend off? I'm only living two hours away."

"I . . . I may be on call."

"Growing up you said you'd always be there for me, Kate. I don't have anyone else. We're kind of kindred spirits in that regard."

"What about your mom?"

"She died last Christmas."

A lump formed in Kate's throat. "I'm sorry, Tina."

"So am I. You deserve an apology. What came out after Eddie's death . . . I should have believed you."

The last thing Kate wanted was to open old wounds concerning Tina's brother. "Where are you?"

"Mercy, Georgia. About two hours north of Atlanta. I'm a housekeeper for a man named Nolan Price and his teenage daughter. I needed a job. Nolan was kind enough to take me in."

"Listen, Tina, I don't think —"

"Remember your grandfather's cross?"

How could Kate forget? Of all things to give Eddie as a token of her love, handing him her most cherished possession three years ago had been the most foolish.

"I found the cross in Eddie's safety-deposit box," Tina said. "Just like my brother to tuck it away."

Kate's shoulders slumped with relief. The cross hadn't been destroyed in the fire.

Her grandfather's face floated through her mind — the man who'd loved her, raised her, taught her about a God she had eventually shut out of her life.

"I'll give you the cross tonight. You can stay the weekend and see for yourself what I'm talking about."

Kate shook her head ever so slightly. "Sounds like you're trying to blackmail me into visiting you."

Tina laughed, a self-deprecating sound that for an instant touched Kate's heart. "Call it a bribe, okay?"

Kate sighed. Bribery or not, she needed the cross back around her neck. Sure, Tina could mail it to her, but Kate wouldn't risk losing the cross again.

"Give me directions," she finally said.

"Take the connector to 400 North."

Jamming the phone between her ear and shoulder, Kate reached into the pocket of her lab coat. She pulled out a small tablet and ballpoint pen and jotted down the instructions.

"Tell me what you *think* you discovered, Tina."

"Not over the phone. You've got to see it. With your scientific background, you'll know if it's worth my getting worried."

You already are, Kate wanted to say. "Surely there's someone else who can help you."

"I don't know who to trust."

"The police?"

"No!"

"You're scaring me, Tina."

"Yeah. I know. That's the way I feel. Scared to death."

Kate hadn't wanted the phone call from Tina, hadn't expected it. Yet, here she was zooming along a desolate back road, heading into rural North Georgia on the coldest day in February to meet a woman she never thought she'd see again.

Dark clouds rolled across the evening sky and added to the anxiety eating at her ever since she'd heard Tina's voice. Usually the levelheaded pragmatist, Kate had done an about-face. Driving into an approaching storm to revisit a friendship that probably should remain dead didn't make sense.

Her cherished cross was the only reason she had agreed to meet Tina. Ever since she'd given it to Eddie, her life had fallen apart, as though God had left her when she'd parted with the necklace. Maybe retrieving the cross would turn her life around. Right now she'd do anything to get back on track.

She looked at the empty can of diet soda perched in her car's console. Too much caffeine and too little sleep over the last few days working on her research project had taken its toll.

Now she had two weeks to kill.

She'd meet Tina, get the cross and find a B and B on the way back to Atlanta. A good dinner and a soak in a hot tub sounded like a fit ending to a long day. About twelve hours of sleep were just what she needed.

Kate reached into her handbag and grabbed a bottle of antacid tablets. She could imagine her boss's voice. "You'll kill yourself before your thirtieth birthday." Jason Bannister often teased her about her marathon work habits. Probably the most savvy scientist Kate had ever worked for, Jason had hired her six months ago for research and development, confident she would succeed.

The partnership study with Southern Technology would have put Bannister Scientific on the map in diabetes research and ensured the two companies merged into the largest laboratory in the southeast.

Except the clinical trials hadn't supported Southern Technology's data. The newspaper article only compounded the problem.

Kate shouldn't have talked to the reporter. She'd had a lapse in judgment, which was something she didn't accept in others, and certainly not in herself.

She shook her head. She and Tina were

14

exact opposites in that regard.

Tina saw the good, ignored the bad. Maybe that was why it hurt so much when her once-upon-a-time friend had cut Kate out of her life.

Kate glanced at her reflection in the rear-view mirror. Even Tina's raven-black hair and voluptuous Latina body contrasted sharply with Kate's rather average looks. In Kate's opinion, her only attributes — and that might be stretching the point — were her fierce determination and blue eyes. Right now those eyes were bloodshot-red.

A roll of thunder forced her attention back to the road as twilight faded into night. Kate switched on the Mustang's headlights and took a left at the four-way stop. So far, she'd had no problem following Tina's directions, but the descending darkness and plummeting temperature threatened to make the last segment of the journey more challenging.

What had brought Tina to this isolated spot? A job? Nothing indicated the area was inhabited other than a few mailboxes by the side of the road and driveways that twisted into oblivion behind the tall pine trees.

Lightning flashed across the sky. Seconds later, a crash of thunder sounded as if it hit the edge of the road. All around her the pine trees danced, their groans mixing with the whistling wind.

A fine mist turned to drizzle. Kate clicked on the wipers and checked to make sure her window was closed tight, then shoved the heater knob to high.

A road sign warned of a sharp curve. Kate downshifted and felt the powerful engine slip into Second. From what Tina had said, a bridge crossed Mercy Creek just ahead.

The rain strengthened. Fat drops splashed against the windshield. A blast of wind hit full force. Kate gripped the wheel to keep the car from crossing the yellow line. As the wind surge died, she flipped the wipers to high and scanned the road for the bridge. The turnoff to Tina's should be on the far side of the creek.

From out of nowhere, a deer charged into the beam of her headlights. Kate pushed in the clutch and stomped on the brake while her hand shoved the gear into First. The tires squealed in protest as the car skidded across the road.

The animal hit the front bumper with a loud thump, soared in the air and crashed against her windshield.

The massive carcass blocked Kate's view. Instinctively, she turned against the skid. The deer shifted to the passenger's side, smearing a bloody trail along the windshield.

Her heart slammed against her chest.

The Mustang was headed for the creek.

The car broke through the guardrail. A jagged edge of steel grated against the door, ripping a gash in the passenger side. For half a second, the auto teetered on the edge of the bridge, then plunged into the raging current below.

Kate screamed. Ice-cold water rushed in like a tsunami, flooding everything in its path.

She floated somewhere outside the realm of consciousness until a searing pain in her leg and bone-chilling cold snapped her back to reality. Where was she?

Try to think. The car, a deer, the bridge . . .

Oh, dear God.

Water swirled around her knees. She couldn't feel her left leg, couldn't move it. The right one throbbed with pain.

Get out. Kate unbuckled her seat belt and pushed on the driver's door. Locked. She reached for the button to release the latch, grabbed the handle and shoved. Nothing budged.

She tried the automatic window. A grinding noise filled the car, and the glass lowered ever so slightly.

"Help me," she shouted through the crack. The wind caught her words and erased them from the night.

She wanted to cry, but she was too terrified, and there was no time. She had to free herself.

Dipping her hand into the swirling eddy, she grabbed her cell phone from the console and shook out the water. Kate pushed the power button. No light. No start-up jingle.

The rain pounded against the car with an unrelenting fury. The water continued to rise. Waist high. Cold. Dark. Her teeth chattered as she gasped for air. *Don't panic.*

She smashed the cell phone against the window, hoping to break the glass. Crash-resistant silicon proved stronger than cellular technology. Enraged, Kate threw the phone against the far window and heard the plunk as it dropped into the pool of water filling the car.

The horn.

She hit the center of the wheel. A momentary blare erupted, then sputtered out like a dying engine.

This couldn't be happening.

"Oh, please." She pushed on the door with all her strength, but it wouldn't move.

A sound cut through the storm.

She strained to hear. The wind howled

and thunder rumbled.

Nothing.

Maybe a hallucination from hypothermia.

Numb. That was how she felt. Not cold. Not hot. It wouldn't be long. As much as she needed to hold on to hope, death seemed inevitable.

But giving up had never been her style.

What had she read? People didn't respond to calls for help.

"Fire," she screamed through the opening in the window as she continued to push against the door. "Help me. Fire. Help me. Fire." She repeated the sequence until her voice cracked and finally gave out just like the horn.

Tears streamed down her face and mixed with the water now at chest level. Soon her mouth would be covered, then her nose. How long before death would take her? Two minutes? Three?

God, help me.

A speck of light flickered through the darkness.

"Here I am," Kate cried out, her voice weak even to her own ears. She hit the horn. Nothing.

The light zigzagged through the tall pines. Too far away to see her. She had to make some sound.

Her right leg broke free from the tangled metal of the brake pedal. She raised her foot and strained to reach the shoe that slipped through her outstretched fingers. She lunged. A driving pain sliced through her left leg. Kate shoved her hand deeper into the water and caught the heel of her pump. Raising the shoe to the windshield, she pounded against the glass.

A dull thud filled the night. Would anyone hear her signal for help?

The light disappeared.

Water lapped around her neck, but she wouldn't give up. Over and over again, she slammed the shoe against the window.

Slowly, warmth engulfed her, as if the water temperature had risen twenty degrees. A sense of euphoria swept over her. She was swimming in her old neighborhood pool. Tina sat on the edge of the deep end next to Eddie with his broad shoulders and lifeguard tan. Kate smiled, waved and . . .

Something jarred her. The door wrenched open. Hands touched her.

"It's okay. I've got you now."

A man pulled her from the car. Her head fell against his shoulder.

"Hold on, honey."

Instinctively, she clung to him. "Eddie?"

They were moving. Going through the

water, but Kate felt nothing except the strength of his embrace. She wanted to drift to sleep in his arms.

"Stay with me," his voice warned.

Suddenly, she was lying on the cold, hard ground. Rain pelted her face.

She blinked her eyes open.

Eddie hadn't saved her. Someone else had.

He dropped to the ground beside her and lifted her into his arms.

"I know this hurts," he said.

She pushed her hands against his massive chest, but he drew her closer. "No!"

She couldn't move. With one hand, he held her tight against his body. With the other, he reached for something. A heavy wool coat wrapped over them, and he hunkered down under its protection.

A siren wailed in the distance. Kate heard it, or thought she did. Only partially aware of the sound, she was totally aware of the man holding her close.

Her eyes were heavy. She wanted to sleep, but his gentle voice urged her to stay with him.

"Don't leave me," he said over and over again, as if they were a team working together to keep her alive.

A chorus of voices broke through the night.

"Over here," he yelled. "North side of the creek."

Help was coming. But Kate didn't want to leave the protection of his embrace.

"What happened?"

"She went off the bridge. Hypothermia. Keep her warm."

Blankets covered her. Kate felt their weight at the same time he pulled out of her grasp. She shivered, unable to control the spasmodic jerking of her muscles.

"She's in shock."

He touched her hand. "I'll follow the ambulance to the clinic. Is there someone I can call? Maybe a relative?"

She swallowed, tried to speak. Her voice came out a whisper, cracked. "Call Tina Esp—"

He gasped. "Tina Espinosa?"

Kate nodded.

"Later."

She shook her head. "Now. Let Tina know I'm hurt. She'll help me."

"Tell her, Price," a voice demanded.

Price? The man Tina worked for. Kate latched on to his arm and wouldn't let go.

Another voice chimed in from the foot of the stretcher. "Truth is, ma'am, Tina —"

Sounds swirled around Kate. What had he said?

"Hush!" Nolan glared at the person who had spoken.

Kate gripped her rescuer's hand even tighter. "What happened to Tina?"

Nolan bent down, his face close to hers. Dark eyes, brow wrinkled with concern.

"Tell me," she pleaded.

"I'm . . . I'm sorry," he finally said. "They found her a few hours ago. Tina's dead."

TWO

Nolan Price would rather be anywhere than outside Mercy MedClinic's emergency room. Hand him a financial portfolio to study or a corporate merger to broker and he was home free. But tubes pumping blood and oxygen into dying patients gave him the creeps.

Maybe it was the memories. Eight months and the pain hadn't gone away. He doubted it ever would.

He glanced at his watch — 10:00 p.m. Over three hours since he'd pulled the woman from the creek. Surely medical science, even in this rural facility, could determine the extent of her injuries in that length of time.

Kate Murphy. He'd finally learned her name.

Nolan shook his head. Too much had happened in one afternoon. The phone call about Tina, and then her friend had almost

24

died in his arms.

God had a strange sense of timing.

Of course, he'd found that out with his wife's tragic death.

At least he still had Heather. Not that raising a fifteen-year-old single-handed was anything but tough. Every time he thought he was making headway, she retreated into her shell. He couldn't relate to his daughter no matter how hard he tried. Or prayed.

Maybe they should have stayed in Los Angeles.

He sighed, then pulled his cell from his pocket, hit the home listing and listened as the phone rang and rang.

The answering machine clicked on. "I'm sorry we're unable to take your call. Please leave a message. . . ."

Why wouldn't she answer?

"Heather, I know you're there. Pick up the phone."

No response.

"I'm not mad." Anymore, he wanted to add.

If only Olivia were alive.

"Make sure the doors to the house are locked, and don't open for anyone. I'll be home as soon as I can."

Nolan snapped the phone shut and shoved it back in his pocket as the sheriff pushed through the emergency-room doors. Early forties, tall and lanky, Wayne Turner was a pack-a-day smoker with a habit of poking his nose into everyone else's business.

"Doc said he'd be finished with her soon. Lady's lucky. Tore one of her knee ligaments. That's the extent of it 'cept for a few cuts and scrapes."

Nolan nodded. No reason to encourage Turner. Tonight of all nights, he didn't feel like making conversation.

"Must be quite a lady from what the EMTs said." The sheriff stuck his chin in the air. "What's your take?"

"Last I saw, she was bone cold and struggling to survive. We didn't have time to exchange pleasantries."

Turner shoved his hand in his pocket and rattled his change. "Lucky you found her. The way your house sits back from the road, no way you could have heard the crash. How'd you happen to be outside on a night like this?"

A vision flashed through Nolan's head — Heather's boyfriend running through the woods.

"I was on my way back from talking to Wade Green over at the funeral home about how to handle Tina's arrangements," Nolan said, purposely not mentioning the boy.

"That's when I saw the break in the bridge."

Turner sniffed. "Sorry about your housekeeper. Guess we owe you. Would have been two dead-on-arrivals if you hadn't happened by in the nick of time."

Nolan leaned against the cold tile wall. He hadn't thought of saving anyone when he'd raced after the boy. Then he'd seen the car, realized someone was trapped inside. Thankfully, he'd had his cell phone and the EMTs had answered his call for help or Turner's statement might have proven true.

The Good Lord supposedly didn't give you more than you could handle. Heather was the problem. Tina had filled a portion of the void Olivia left. His daughter confided in the housekeeper, trusted her. Now that Tina was gone, Heather might withdraw even further from him.

"Shame that housekeeper of yours had a flat on Old Man Hawkins' dirt road. Pretty isolated stretch. No one to help her." Turner shook his head. "Allergic to latex. Who'd figure? Not the way I'd wanna die."

Doc Samuels had filled Nolan in earlier. Changing the tire had brought Tina into contact with something that had triggered an anaphylactic reaction.

Ignoring the sheriff, Nolan turned to face the doc as he pushed open the ER doors.

Short, stocky, with a receding hairline and a small birthmark over his left brow, Mercy's sole physician stuck out his hand. "Thanks for staying, Nolan."

He returned the handshake. "Lloyd."

"Good job with the accident victim. Few seconds longer and she'd be in the morgue instead of the treatment room. Keeping her warm did the trick."

"Hypothermia's easy enough to spot."

"Yeah, but you reacted." The doc pointed to the doors he had just stepped through. "That little lady owes you her life."

Nolan shrugged off the praise. "Right time, right place."

"She tore her ACL. Probably won't need surgery, but her leg's too swollen to be sure. She'll need an MRI once the swelling subsides. Right now, I've got her in a knee immobilizer, but she has to stay off her feet for a few days. Problem is her insurance won't cover keeping her here all night. Closest hotel's in Summerton. Don't know if driving over the mountain would be the safest bet." He looked at the sheriff.

"Rain turned to sleet about an hour ago," Turner said. "Highway patrol plans to close the pass to Summerton. The way the temperature's dropping, we'll be iced over for the rest of the night."

"Would Edith mind if —"

Turner held up one hand, palm out. "Count me out, Doc. Edith's spending the night with Ms. Agnes. That handicapped daughter of hers took a turn for the worse. Edith's helping out."

Nolan let out an exasperated breath. Last thing he wanted was a stranger underfoot, but the woman needed a place to stay.

"Kate Murphy knew Tina. Heather and I can put her up until the storm passes."

"Appreciate it," Lloyd said, slapping Nolan's arm. "I gave her something for the pain. She's a little groggy. Check on her occasionally in the night."

The doc turned to the chief. "Ms. Murphy asked about her car."

Turner whistled. "Boys are still trying to pull that sucker out of the water. Probably late morning before the roads improve so they can tow it over to Mercy Automotive. Mind if I get a little info from the patient, Doc?"

Lloyd nodded and pointed the sheriff toward the treatment room.

When Turner was out of earshot, Nolan said, "I talked to the funeral director earlier this evening. Wade said to ask you when Tina's body would be released."

"Already done. Wade picked her up about

an hour ago."

"Thanks, Lloyd."

The doc pointed to the ambulance entrance. "Pull your car around. I'll have the nurse escort Ms. Murphy out in a few minutes."

Nolan parked his Explorer in front of the ER. The sleet had stopped, but ice covered the landscape. Talk about a night to remember.

He left the engine running and the heater on high. Rounding the vehicle, Nolan waited until the automatic doors opened and the nurse wheeled her patient into the cold night.

Wrapped in a white thermal blanket with her left leg propped up, Kate Murphy reminded him of a rag doll that had lost part of its stuffing. She was pale skinned and blurry eyed, as if the life had drained from her.

He opened the back passenger door.

"Can you lift her?" the nurse asked. "I'll stabilize her leg."

Nolan slipped one arm around Kate's shoulders, the other under her knees and raised her from the chair. Light, maybe too light.

She stiffened in his arms and groaned.

"Sorry," he mumbled.

The nurse climbed into the SUV and supported the braced leg as Nolan positioned Kate on the seat.

He could only imagine how she felt.

Hurt. Alone. In the arms of a stranger.

"My daughter's at home," he offered as reassurance, though he felt certain Lloyd had explained the situation. "There's a guest room on the first floor."

"Thank you," she whispered.

The nurse wrapped a second blanket around Kate's body, then stepped out of the car, slammed the door and handed Nolan a typed form. "That leg will bother her for a few days. Ice should help. Everything's in the discharge papers."

"Right."

Nolan climbed into the driver's seat and glanced at his passenger huddled in the rear. As soon as possible, he'd send Kate Murphy back to Atlanta.

He didn't want to be responsible for another woman with what was happening in Mercy.

Kate wrapped the hospital blanket around her shoulders and tried to settle into the backseat of the SUV. Her leg burned like fire, and her body ached as if she'd done a mega workout and pushed every muscle to the limit.

She caught Nolan glancing back at her in the rearview mirror. Dark eyes, pensive, brooding.

"Warm enough?" he asked.

"I'm fine."

She yanked the blanket higher. Her wet clothes were piled in a plastic bag on the floor along with a very soggy wallet someone had found wedged in her car's console. The hospital gown afforded her some modesty, the blankets provided warmth and her credit cards weren't floating downstream. At least there were some things for which to be thankful.

She flicked her gaze back to her rescuer. He appeared tall with jet-black hair, cut close, and piercing eyes that seemed to burn into her whenever he looked her way. He wore a pullover sweater and jeans, and from the looks of his dry clothes, he'd evidently changed after his dip in the creek.

Glancing down at her blanket-swathed body, she was grateful ERs didn't provide mirrors for their patients. She'd hate to see herself. Limp brown hair, faded hospital gown, bags under her eyes, no doubt. Whatever the long-term diagnosis, she knew it wasn't pretty.

Outside the car window, ice covered the

trees and shrubs, every leaf and branch frozen in place. Another time and the landscape would have seemed magical. Like a winter wonderland. But not tonight. After all that had happened, there was nothing magical about Mercy.

The doctor had assured her she'd be comfortable staying at Nolan Price's home. A widower with a teenage daughter. The man Tina had mentioned. Nice of him to take her in. Still, she'd give anything to be home in Atlanta.

Her eyes grew heavy. The doctor had given her something for pain. "To take the edge off," he'd said.

She needed to ask something before she fell asleep. "What . . . What happened to Tina?"

Intent on driving, Nolan apparently hadn't heard her, and she was too tired to repeat the question.

She closed her eyes, and her body floated as if she were in the creek again. This time the sun was shining down, warming her. She drifted. . . .

His hands nudged her.

She opened her eyes.

"Easy does it," he said, hoisting her into his arms. A sharp jab cut through her leg.

A large forbidding structure loomed ahead

of them. Two-story. Brick. No light inviting them in from the cold.

Trees crowded around the house and creaked in the frigid air like old bones dancing in the night.

Kate shivered. This wasn't the welcoming lodge she'd envisioned.

She closed her eyes. A key turned. She blinked. A young girl peered around the open door.

"Kate, this is my daughter, Heather."

Shoulder-length blond hair, petite, big eyes that stared back at her.

"Heather, Miss Murphy's staying in the guest room."

Kate opened her mouth to say hello, but he rushed her past the girl too quickly.

A bed, blankets . . . Kate snuggled down in the warmth, vaguely aware of her host bustling about to get her settled.

Eventually, he placed a pillow under her left leg and a plastic bag filled with ice on top.

Cool, soothing.

"Call me if you need anything," he said.

"Thanks." She tried to smile.

A light flicked off. Darkness enveloped her. She closed her eyes. . . .

Later, the door clicked open.

He bent over her, removed the melted ice

bag and replaced it with a fresh one.

She slept again.

Her grandfather's face floated through her dreams. "No coincidences," he told her. "Only God-incidences."

She wanted to laugh.

Had God brought her to Mercy to find the cross? Or to find Tina?

Then she remembered.

Tina's dead. The words hammered through her brain.

Her eyes flew open. A girl's voice cut through the night. Heather sounded as if she was standing directly outside Kate's room.

"Is she taking Tina's place?"

"I told you, she's only staying a short time."

"But when *I* tell *you* something you never believe me," the girl threw back at her father.

"You know the rules, Heather. No one comes into the house when I'm not home."

"Jimmy stayed outside."

"Then why'd he run away?"

Maybe all families were the same. Kate and her dad had had their share of problems before he'd walked out of her life.

The irony was she was still waiting for him to return.

"I love you, honey." At least Nolan was trying.

"You didn't love Mom."

"Heather, please —"

Too private for Kate's ears. She cleared her throat, hoping they would hear her and take their discussion elsewhere.

"I told you not to leave." The girl's voice was edged with pain. "I knew something bad would happen."

"Your mother's death wasn't my fault, Heather."

"No? Then whose fault was it?"

THREE

Tick. Tick. Tick.

Kate opened her eyes to the gray winter light peering through the curtain, turned her head on the pillow and squinted at the travel alarm perched on the bedside table. Her temples throbbed in sync with the ticking clock.

Eight-fifteen. Later than she'd slept in the last six months.

So why'd she still feel groggy? Probably the drugs Dr. Samuels had given her yesterday at the clinic.

She closed her eyes and started to drift back to sleep. Visions flashed through her mind — the deer, the bridge, the raging water rushing in around her.

Her eyes jerked open. The water receded, replaced by the memory of Nolan's powerful arms and warm embrace. If he hadn't saved her —

Don't go there. Nolan *had* saved her.

Thank God.

She shook her head ever so slightly. Far as she was concerned, God had nothing to do with it.

But Tina? Tears stung Kate's eyes. She blinked them away.

Heather's angry voice echoed in Kate's mind.

Had she imagined the father-daughter spat? Maybe a dream?

A widower trying to raise a teenage daughter had to be tough. Yet, he'd taken Kate into his home.

As much as she appreciated his hospitality, she needed to get up, assess her situation and head back to Atlanta. Back to —

She sighed. Back to an empty condo and two weeks of worry. Until the board of review made their decision.

No telling the outcome.

Headstrong. That was what Jason had called her. Talking to the reporter had been a foolish mistake. She'd put her position and the lab in jeopardy.

Don't cry over spilled milk. Her grandfather's words flowed through her consciousness. Grandda with his Old World practicality. He'd be the first to tell her to focus on the problem at hand.

Cautiously, she eased her arm from under

the down comforter and rubbed her fore-head. If only the jackhammer pounding through her brain would stop.

Mouth as dry as cotton batting, she ran her parched tongue over chapped lips as her eyes swept the room in the half light.

Oak dresser. Ladder-back chair. A roughly hewn wooden cross nailed to the wall next to an oval mirror.

Closet and two other doors. One hung open, exposing a porcelain sink and shower stall, as inviting as a desert oasis.

She threw back the covers, rolled to her side and gasped. A jolt of white lightning sliced through her left leg.

"Argh!" Falling back on the bed, Kate fought the wave of nausea that rolled over her along with the frigid morning air.

An empty stomach and pain medication didn't mix. She hadn't eaten since breakfast yesterday — one low-fat granola bar washed down with coffee.

Sucking in a few shallow puffs of air, she waited until the pain subsided, then slowly rose to a sitting position and examined the immobilizer secured around her left leg with Velcro straps. A torn ACL.

Kate didn't have time for another problem.

Determined to push through the pain, she

eased herself to the edge of the bed and carefully lowered her feet to the cold hardwood floor. Putting weight on her good leg, she stood upright.

The room faded into darkness. Kate grabbed the nightstand and waited for her sudden drop in blood pressure to pass. Poised precariously like a flamingo on one foot, she winced as her hurt leg fought against her effort and blinked the room back into focus.

She wouldn't run any marathons today. Five hops to the bathroom might be more than she could manage.

Trading the support of the nightstand for the dresser, she inched across the room. With every movement, her leg screamed in protest. Finally, she reached the bathroom, slumped against the sink and held her breath until the stabbing pain eased.

Kate glanced at the face looking back at her from the mirror.

Sunken eyes. Pale skin. Twisted matt of hair.

She flipped on the wall switch and sighed when the light failed to work. Electricity must have gone out in the night.

Reaching for the faucet, she turned on the water, lowered her head and gulped the cool liquid pooled in her outstretched hand.

A travel kit of wrapped toiletries sat on the basin. She jabbed a fingernail into the cellophane, grabbed a pocket comb and raked it through her hair, then brushed her teeth, scrubbed her face and toweled dry. What she wouldn't give for a shower.

Her eyes once again connected with the stranger in the mirror. Not her best day by a long shot.

A white terry-cloth robe hung on a wall hook. Kate snuggled into the thick cotton, left the bathroom and hobbled to the guest-room door.

What would she find on the other side?

Sucking in a fortifying breath, she reached for the knob and pulled. Stairs climbed upward directly outside her room. She grabbed the banister for support and examined the hallway around her.

Photos hung on the wall. Nolan arm in arm with his daughter. A second picture of Heather when she was a little girl. A third of Tina and Nolan sitting side by side at a kitchen table.

Older, more mature, but Tina still flaunted the flirtatious smile and laughing eyes.

A life cut short. Why? Kate's mind swirled. So senseless.

She let go of the stair railing, reached for the wall and misjudged the distance.

Her right knee buckled. She tumbled forward.

From out of nowhere, arms grabbed her. Pulled her upright.

Kate twisted and stared into Nolan's dark eyes.

He raised an eyebrow. "You should have called for help."

"I didn't expect another crash. Seems you've saved me a second time."

The corner of his mouth twitched. "You prone to trouble?"

"Not usually." She found her footing, straightened her shoulders and tried to gracefully extract herself from his hold. "I'm fine."

"Really? Looks to me like you're ready to keel over."

Exactly how she felt. Her blood pressure must be ninety over fifty, the way her head was swimming.

His hands continued to steady her. "Lean against me for support."

Embarrassed to appear so needy, Kate put weight on her injured leg, then gasped as a hot slice of pain shot through her knee.

Swallow your pride, Kate.

If Nolan wanted to help, why not let him? The world could use a few more heroes.

His arm slid around her waist. "Easy does it."

Slowly, he guided her through the doorway and into the welcoming interior of the great room. A blazing fire crackled a greeting from a massive stone fireplace on the far wall.

Nolan lowered her into a leather chair, warm from someone's previous body heat. A half-full cup of coffee sat on the side table. Nolan's chair.

"Listen, I don't want to take your —"

"Would you *please* sit down?" His tone was firm. Then he smiled. "You always so obstinate?"

"My grandfather called me stubborn."

"I'd have to agree with him."

Kate wiggled back into the deep cushions as Nolan raised her left leg to the ottoman and covered it with a chenille throw he grabbed off the couch. He tucked the covering around her bare foot before he stood and surveyed his patient.

A sense of gratitude spread over Kate. "I can't thank you enough. You saved my life last night. Then you took me in. Now you're waiting on me hand and foot." She glanced down at her injured leg. "*Literally.* I'm not used to such treatment."

"Chalk it up to Southern hospitality.

coffee?"

"A little sweetener."

"Sugar okay?"

"Of course." She wove her fingers into the folds of the throw. "I really do appreciate your generosity."

"Not a problem. Besides, you knew Tina." He shook his head and swallowed. "Still can't believe it. Tina was a good employee and a friend to Heather." He sighed. "My daughter and I are both having a hard time."

"Death's tough on everyone."

Nolan's eyes softened. "Were you and Tina old friends?"

"Since grammar school. The Espinosas lived next door."

"Guess you heard, Tina's mom passed away last December. No other living relatives. Her brother died three years ago."

"I knew about Eddie." Kate lowered her gaze, hoping her eyes didn't reflect the pain written on her heart.

"Funny, Tina never mentioned having a friend in Atlanta."

Kate pulled in a steadying breath. "We'd been out of touch for a few years."

"Bad timing, huh?"

She jerked her head up. "What?"

"Arriving in town the day she died. Must

be tearing you apart."

How *did* she feel? Regret? Sorrow? Three years and Kate couldn't get past the rejection.

"So what brought you to Mercy?" Nolan asked.

"Tina had something that belonged to me. Did she ever mention a gold cross?"

"Not that I recall. Then again, she kept personal matters to herself. Lived in the apartment over the garage." His eyes flicked over Kate's injured leg. "Stairs are steep. Don't suggest you go poking around up there."

"Of course not." Had Tina told Nolan about what she'd seen in the woods? She'd said she didn't trust anyone. Did that include her boss?

"I'll talk to Heather. Maybe she's seen the cross. If we find it, we'll be sure to give it back to you." Nolan pointed toward the kitchen door. "I'll get that coffee now."

Kate watched him leave. On the surface, he seemed like a nice enough guy, and he'd saved her life, for which she'd be eternally grateful. But she needed to be careful. People weren't always who they seemed.

She shook her head. *Lighten up, would you?*

Better to focus on the positive.

Kate gazed around the room. Framed

45

photos of Heather sat on the mantel. Tough raising a child alone.

Even harder for a girl who needed a mother's love. Kate should know. God had robbed her of that luxury, too.

Maybe that was why Tina's mom had played such an important roll in Kate's life.

Until the fire had changed their relationship forever.

Kate shook her head, blocking the memory from returning full force. Not today. She had too much to deal with as it was. No need to dredge up the past.

She glanced at the windows to her right. Thick burgundy drapes, held back with tassels, let in a glimpse of the frozen world outside.

In front of her a leather-bound Bible lay open on the coffee table as if Nolan had stopped midverse to tend to her needs.

A door creaked. Kate turned at the sound. Nolan entered the room, along with the mouthwatering smell of sausage and eggs. He set the tray on the coffee table. "I kept breakfast warm for you. Hungry?"

"A bit. Thank you."

She accepted the plate he offered. A wedge of melon, two sausage patties, scrambled eggs, biscuits. Not her usual fare and far more appealing than a dry breakfast bar. "You must be a miracle maker. Isn't the power out?"

"I've got a gas stove. Comes in handy in this type of weather. And a small generator that works the water pump. I keep a stove-top coffeemaker for these occasions, as well." He placed a glass of orange juice and mug of coffee on the side table.

The rich aroma made her stomach churn, reminding her she hadn't eaten in over twenty-four hours.

He shuffled his feet and glanced at the door he'd just walked through. "Holler if you need anything. I'll be in the kitchen cleaning up."

Kate reached for the silverware as he left the room and shoved a forkful of eggs into her mouth.

"Mmm." The man could cook.

When she finished, she placed the empty plate on the table, closed her eyes and dozed until a knock caused her eyes to fly open. She straightened in the chair and listened.

Heavy steps crossed the hardwood foyer. A door opened.

"Doc." Nolan's voice. "Didn't think you'd be able to make it over this morning. How're the roads?"

"Could be better. Thank goodness for four-wheel drive."

"Let me hang up your coat."

Fabric rustled. She envisioned the doctor shrugging out of his wrap.

"How's my patient?"

"Resting. She ate breakfast earlier."

Kate glanced at the side table. The dirty dishes had been replaced with a second glass of juice.

"Still deathly pale," Nolan continued, his voice drawing closer.

She raked her hand through her hair, a bit self-conscious at being the topic of their discussion.

The door to the foyer opened. Lloyd Samuels burst into the room, bringing a rush of cool air with him.

"Morning, Kate. Looks like Nolan's taking good care of you."

She glanced from the doctor to her host and smiled. "He's been very kind."

"The nurse forgot to give you these last night." He placed the wooden crutches he carried on the floor beside her chair. "Should help your mobility. Glad to see you've got that leg elevated."

Reaching for the chenille throw, he asked, "Mind if I take a peek?"

"Not at all." Kate flipped the cover off her left leg and looked up.

Nolan's eyes locked on hers. She flushed

and looked away.

"I'll give you two some privacy." Nolan stepped toward the kitchen door. "Coffee, Lloyd?"

"Sounds good. Add a little cream, if you've got it."

The doctor bent to examine Kate's leg. Unfastening the brace, his fingers probed a tender spot. She drew in a sharp breath.

"Sorry. Swelling's about the same. Use the crutches and keep your weight off that leg for a few more days."

"I need to get back to Atlanta."

"Not until the swelling goes down." He reconnected the immobilizer, then fished a plastic bottle from his pocket and placed it on the table. "Pain medication. I called in a prescription to the pharmacy. These'll tide you over until the roads clear. Sheriff said the electricity should be on later this evening. By tomorrow morning, things should be back to normal."

A two-hour drive from Atlanta with a wrecked auto and injured leg, Kate doubted *her* life would be normal anytime soon. She'd give herself seventy-two hours max to recuperate here in Mercy. Then, she'd return to Atlanta one way or another.

Nolan returned with mugs of coffee and offered one to the doctor, who sipped the hot brew and smacked his lips. "Just what I needed."

He downed another swig before looking thoughtfully at Nolan. "Where's Heather?"

"Upstairs. She refuses to leave her room."

The doctor nodded. "Kids have a hard time accepting death, especially when it's sudden. I could prescribe something."

"No."

The sharpness of Nolan's response surprised Kate, although she had to agree. Drugs wouldn't help Heather deal with her grief.

"I know how much Tina meant to Heather." Doc Samuels cleared his throat. "Like I told you at the clinic, Kate, folks in Mercy loved Tina. She was a committed Christian with a good heart."

Last night, Kate's mind had been fuzzy with pain medication. Had she told the doctor about Tina's phone call? Surely, Lloyd Samuels wasn't one of the people Tina had said she couldn't trust.

The doctor looked at Nolan. "Wade said he talked to you about holding Tina's service as soon as possible. That is, if the weather cooperates."

Kate readjusted the throw and reached for the coffee Nolan had placed next to her chair.

"You mean Tina's funeral?" she asked, the mug halfway to her lips. "Why the rush?"

"Another storm's expected early next week," the doc replied. "Plus, Mercy's a small town. News travels. No need to wait for the obit notice in the paper. Most folks work during the week. More of them would be able to pay their respects tomorrow."

Nolan raised his brow. "Tomorrow?"

"That's right. Wade wants to take advantage of the lull between the storms."

Kate slanted another glance out the window. "Isn't the ground frozen?"

"Not a problem." The doctor drank again.

She imagined the frigid air blowing over the gravesite. "But —"

He placed the mug on the table and smiled. "Cremation, Miss Murphy. That's what Tina requested."

Cremation? No way.

Blame it on a Hispanic upbringing, but cremation had never been an option for the Espinosa family. Eddie's death had only driven home the point.

Never by fire. Never.

Kate needed to set the doctor straight. "Look, cremation's not what Tina would have wanted."

"According to Wade, it's precisely what she *did* want," the doctor insisted.

"You're saying she prearranged her funeral?"

"Not exactly. But she and Wade talked once Tina realized her condition was life threatening."

"Pardon?"

The doctor's nostrils flared. "So Wade would know her preferences in case something unforeseen happened, Miss Murphy."

His tone was sharp. Maybe he didn't like his authority questioned.

"Tina was only twenty-nine." And never one to plan for the future, Kate remembered, keeping the thought to herself.

Lloyd shrugged. "But highly allergic."

"To what?"

"Latex, Kate. A growing problem. The incidence has increased significantly in the last twenty years or so."

Kate knew the statistics. "Since medical personnel began wearing gloves on a regular basis. But that's within the health-care community."

The doctor turned to Nolan. "Didn't you say Tina worked as a nurse's aide out in California?"

"That's where we met her."

"Told me she'd had contact dermatitis for years," Lloyd continued.

"Eczema," Kate interjected. Tina had

always been self-conscious of her rough red skin. An irritating condition but not the result of latex.

"The situation had progressed recently." The doctor ignored Kate's diagnosis. "Tina had been concerned. And rightfully so."

"And that's what killed her?"

"Seems her car had a blowout on one of the back farm roads. She tried to change the tire. Something triggered a reaction. Maybe the rubber in the tire —" He glanced at Nolan. "Latex is made from rubber."

"A derivative," Kate clarified.

The doctor raised a brow and smirked rather condescendingly down at her. "Sounds like you have a scientific background."

"Chemistry." She didn't mention the completed credit hours for her Ph.D.

"Then you understand anaphylactic shock. Ralph Hawkins found her on his property, called the EMTs. Her heart had stopped long before she arrived at the clinic."

Kate thought of Tina dying all alone on some isolated stretch of country road. Tears welled up in her eyes.

Friends for life. That was what she and Tina had promised one another so long ago.

The doctor reached for the bottle of pills

he'd placed on the side table, shook one into his palm and held it out. "You've been through a lot, Kate. Take this caplet."

She didn't want the pill.

"Come on, now," he insisted. "I can tell you're upset. You need to rest."

She looked from the doctor to Nolan warming himself in front of the fire, his expression impossible to read.

A shiver rolled down Kate's spine as she recalled his daughter's words the night before.

Wife dead.

Tina dead.

The common denominator was Nolan.

What had Kate stumbled into?

She grabbed the glass of juice off the table and threw the pill into her mouth.

The doctor turned to shake Nolan's hand. "Keep me posted on the arrangements."

"Will do. Appreciate your help, Doc."

Without a backward glance at Kate, the two men walked toward the door.

As soon as they left the room, Kate spit the pill into her hand. She didn't need medication to sleep. She needed to keep her eyes wide open. Tina's death didn't add up.

If not latex, then what had killed Tina?

FOUR

Nolan said goodbye to Lloyd, then climbed the stairs to the second floor and stopped outside Heather's bedroom.

"Honey?"

He knocked twice, grabbed the knob and twisted.

Locked.

"Can I bring you something, Heather? A cup of tea? Maybe a sandwich?"

"I'm not hungry," she said, her voice muffled by the closed door.

"The electricity will come on soon, but it's cold up here. You don't want to get sick."

"I'm wearing my jacket."

He pictured her sitting on the canopy bed, bundled in her peacoat and stocking hat, red-eyed and totally confused. Part child, part woman, she waged war with her emotions, trying to stay in control.

Just as she had when Olivia had died.

"I'll make spaghetti for dinner." Heather's

favorite. Hunger might coax her from her seclusion. "Why don't you come down soon?"

No answer.

"You need to eat."

"Not now, Dad." Her voice cracked.

The sound slammed against his heart. His baby was too young to carry her cross alone. If only she'd let him into her pain.

Lord, let me be her Simon of Cyrene.

"See you soon, okay?" He listened for a minute, then turned and walked, heavy-hearted, down the stairs.

The door to the great room hung open. Leather chair empty. Crutches gone.

He knocked on the guest room door. "Miss Murphy . . . Kate, you need any-thing?"

A muffled "No, thank you," reached his ears.

Two females in the house, both hiding behind closed doors. Could give a guy a complex.

"You'll find some ladies' clothing in the closet." He cleared his throat. "A family lost their home in a flood, so Heather and I bought clothes for them. Seems to me, the mother's about your size."

"I couldn't impose —"

"Nonsense. We can buy more next week."

He let out a frustrated breath. Hard to carry on a conversation through an inch and a half of hardwood. "The great room's warm thanks to the fireplace. I could make a spot for you on the couch."

"That's not necessary."

"You'll find a quilt in one of the drawers."

"Thank you, Nolan."

If the woman wanted to hole up in a chilly bedroom rather than enjoy the comfort of the great room, so be it. "Let me know if you need anything."

The bedsprings creaked.

"We'll eat dinner about five. In the kitchen. The oven puts out a good amount of heat. That is, if you can sit at the table comfortably."

"Thanks. I doubt I'll be hungry."

"Makes me think you're worried about my cooking." He forced a laugh, trying to lighten the mood. "I'm not a gourmet, but . . . well . . ."

Suddenly, he was a comedian?

No need to embarrass himself further. "See you later."

"Wait." The door opened. Crutch in hand, Kate scooted forward, propped her shoulder against the wooden doorjamb and let out a ragged breath. Her hair framed her face, cheeks flushed from exertion, brow wrinkled.

"Sorry it took me so long to get to the door." She glanced down at her injured leg. "I'm slow as a tortoise with this injury."

"I shouldn't have disturbed you."

"You didn't. Dinner at five sounds fine. Although after that huge breakfast, I should probably skip a meal or two." She looked up. "You've been very kind."

"All you've been through, the least Heather and I could do was offer you a place to stay. Plus, we have plenty of room."

Kate glanced down the hallway. "And a beautiful home."

He noticed a small puddle of water by the front door, which he pointed out to Kate. "Lloyd must have had ice on his shoes. Tina would have given the doc a piece of her mind for tracking up her hardwoods."

A spark of amusement flickered in Kate's eyes. "Sounds like something she'd do."

"So Tina was a neat freak even as a kid?"

"And put me to shame," Kate said with a laugh. "My idea of clean was to shove everything under my bed and hope no one noticed." She looked at the picture hanging on the wall.

Nolan followed her gaze. Heather had taken the photo a couple weeks after they'd arrived in Mercy while Nolan and Tina had sat at the kitchen table.

"Looks like you two were having fun," Kate finally said.

"Heather wanted to try out her new camera. That little skunk made faces at us until we were both howling with laughter."

One of the first lighthearted moments he and Heather had shared after Olivia's death. He had hung the photo to remind them life went on even after the loss of a loved one.

"Where'd you happen to meet Tina?" Kate asked.

"In California. When Olivia got sick, I needed someone to help with her care. Tina was looking for a new job." He shrugged. "Win-win, all the way around."

"I'm sorry about your wife." She hesitated a moment, then asked, "Was it cancer?"

"Olivia died of an infection. She'd had surgery. I thought she was doing better, but . . ." He sighed, a heavy weight on his chest.

Suddenly, he was tired of talking. "You look like you need some rest. Probably that medicine Lloyd gave you. He's quick to push pills."

"So I noticed. A nap sounds good. See you about five?"

"I'll keep the fire roaring. Come out earlier, if you get cold."

She closed the door as he stepped into the great room and walked to the hearth. Grabbing the poker, he stoked the fire. The flames licked the logs, sending sparks dancing like fireflies in the air.

Once again, the memory of Olivia's declining health swirled around him. Both of them had skirted the real issue of a Hollywood lifestyle gone amok.

Alcohol. Drugs.

Olivia had been so good at explaining away her symptoms that he'd turned a blind eye to the truth, especially when she'd promised the unexpected trip to India would be her last.

A fact-finding expedition for a documentary on the plight of India's poor who sold their organs to rich foreigners — a transplant tourist racket she'd wanted to explore.

Nolan shook his head. Organs for a price.

For Olivia Price.

Only later, he'd learned the truth. She hadn't gone to India to gather information. She'd gone to buy an organ.

He'd never suspected liver disease.

Nolan threw another log on the fire. To Olivia, time was money and too precious to be spent waiting for a donor through normal channels in the States.

So she'd found another way. The unscrupulous physicians at the Beverly Hills Specialty Center had claimed the procedure was as safe abroad as in the U.S. Olivia's mistake had been to trust the upscale medical facility that catered to the rich and famous. Too late, she'd learned they covered up the high rate of complications that often led to death, just as it had with Olivia.

Fisting his hands, anger swelled up in Nolan anew.

Why hadn't she told him the real reason for her trip? Probably because by that point their marriage had been a sham.

On the exterior, they had looked like the perfect family. Except he and Olivia had been living a lie.

Nolan shook his head, sorrow overwhelming him. Justice. That was what he'd expected. Sanjeer Hira and the other physicians at the Beverly Hills Center had preyed on Olivia's fear of not finding a donor in time, but no illegality could be found. Bottom line, the authorities' hands were tied. Despite the dangers, private citizens were free to undergo medical procedures abroad.

Fingers pressed against the mantel, Nolan stared into the fire. When Olivia had told him about a pre-op stop she had made in Georgia, Nolan had realized he might have a way to bring down the Beverly Hills operation and the physicians involved.

A limousine had picked Olivia up at the Atlanta airport and had driven her to a VIP suite in a rural mountain clinic. There she'd received a special IV treatment exclusively for liver patients to increase the rate of recovery. Twelve hours later, she'd been whisked back to Atlanta and had boarded her flight to India.

The fact that the Beverly Hills physicians had insisted she use an alias during her Georgia layover raised a red flag in Nolan's mind. A legit medical procedure wouldn't require cash up front. Nor a fictitious identity for the patient.

Carrying a hefty load of grief and guilt, Nolan had moved to Mercy after Olivia's death. If he couldn't get to the Beverly Hills Center through the front door, he'd go in the back way. Surely, someone in the small Georgia town had made or would make a mistake, exposing a crack in the seemingly flawless Beverly Hills facade.

With dogged determination and hours of surveillance, pieces of the puzzle were falling into place, but the picture appeared more corrupt than he had even imagined.

Now Tina had died.

And her old friend was sleeping in the guest room.

Probably a mistake to offer Kate lodging. Although it *had* been the Christian thing to do. Besides, where else would she have gone? To a hotel in Summerton? The pass had closed, and the last thing Nolan wanted was an innocent woman out on her own.

Dropping into the leather chair, he pulled the Bible to his lap and let his fingers slide over the page.

Maybe he and Heather should shake the dust of Mercy from their feet and move on.

He sighed. Who was he trying to fool?

He couldn't leave until he found a way to expose the transplant tourist racket that had led to Olivia's death.

His eyes focused on a scripture verse.

" 'Beware of false prophets, who come to you in sheep's clothing, but underneath are ravenous wolves.' "

A warning?

Nolan stared into the fire.

Lord, I need your help to find the wolves. All of them.

Kate nestled down in the bed and pulled the comforter up around her neck. How could a quick trip to Mercy, Georgia, to retrieve her grandfather's cross turn into such a disaster?

Tina was dead. The cross was still missing. And Kate was holed up in a house that lacked electricity, tended to by a kind and attractive man.

Not that she wasn't grateful. Better here than out in the cold. Or in some lonely hotel room. Although as she recalled, Dr. Samuels had said Mercy didn't have a hotel.

Small town. One physician.

And what about the doc? He insisted a woman she'd known forever had died of a long-term condition Kate had never heard Tina mention.

Add cremation to the mix. The idea of Tina — a live-for-the-minute type of gal — planning her funeral left a bad taste in Kate's mouth.

Cremation . . . fire . . .

Kate's stomach tightened. The memory of that horrible night three years ago returned unbidden. She closed her eyes, trying to shut out all that had happened.

Trusting and gullible, she had put her faith on the line . . . faith in a man who'd professed to love her . . . faith in a God who, she thought, would bless their love.

Only to have her hopes and dreams go up in flames.

Stupid to believe she and Eddie would live happily ever after. She'd learned the hard way fairy tales don't come true.

She'd been blinded by love. Or had she ignored the signs, not wanting to believe the truth? Living a lie was so much easier.

Until she'd come face-to-face with the reality of his addiction.

The man she'd loved — had thought she'd loved — had transformed before her eyes into a junkie needing the next fix.

The cabin had been Eddie's private retreat, but he'd begged her to drop by just this once. He'd promised to throw steaks on the grill and have her home by nine so she would be ready for work the next day.

That night with candles flicking in the darkness and the cloying, sweet smell of incense hanging in the air, she'd discovered the true Eddie.

She'd entered a den of evil. The words he'd screamed. The names he'd called her.

He'd mocked her values and her morality, calling her a stupid prude who needed to be taught a lesson.

When he'd grabbed at her dress, she'd fought back, needing to escape.

Kate clenched her teeth, eyes scrunched shut as once again she relived the struggle.

Fear gripped her anew.

"Run, Kate, run," an inner voice warned just as it had that night.

In her mind's eye, she tripped, a table

overturned. She crawled forward, struggled to her feet.

Somehow she found the door and ran. Ran from the cabin, from his shouts of protest. Ran until her lungs burned and her muscles ached and she gasped for air.

In that instant, she looked back.

The explosion ripped the night in two.

"Oh, God, no!" she cried into the folds of the comforter. The memory too real, too painful.

Tears spilled from her eyes. Her breath caught in shallow spasms. She raked her fingers through her hair and willed herself to gain control. But she couldn't stop the tears.

She cried for all she had lost that night. For the dreams that had died with Eddie. For the life she'd wanted, had come to expect, that had ended with the fire. For the lie about love she'd believed too long.

She wasn't worthy of love. Love was for those good enough and deserving enough.

She was neither.

Her father had walked out of her life.

Eddie had betrayed her.

She'd learned her lesson. She'd never love again. The pain was too great to bear.

And she'd carried it too long.

"It's okay. I've got you now. Hold on, honey."

Nolan's words when he'd saved her from the water slammed through her mind.

Where had that come from?

Crazy.

She pushed the thought away and pulled in another ragged breath.

She needed to escape from *all* the memories.

Sleep, Kate. Hopefully, she'd find solace in her slumber.

Unless Nolan found his way there.

No. She shook her head. She wouldn't give him access to her dreams . . . or her emotions.

That was a promise she had to keep.

By 5:00 p.m., the pungent mix of sausage, tomatoes and Italian seasonings filled the kitchen. Nolan stirred the sauce simmering on the stove and waited for water in the large stainless steel pot to boil.

Dark skies hung outside the kitchen window as desolate as his mood. Ice that had begun to melt midday had refrozen with the evening drop in temperature.

Earlier, he'd walked the property, passed the creek where Kate's car had broken through the guardrail then plummeted into the icy water below.

The Almighty had directed his steps.

Thank You, Lord. Otherwise two women would need to be laid to rest.

Hard to believe Tina was dead. And from a reaction to latex. It didn't make sense.

If only Tina had been more forthcoming about her condition. She'd been so private, and Nolan hadn't wanted to pry.

Kate had questioned cremation. But Tina didn't have much money, and cremation was a cheaper option for her. Nolan shook his head. Right now, he needed to focus on Heather.

With a heavy heart, he stirred the sauce and glanced at his watch. Thirty minutes ago, he'd rapped on Heather's door and told her dinner was almost ready. Not that he expected his daughter to leave her room.

If only Kate would come out soon, trade her afternoon of seclusion for a good meal and a little conversation.

A smiling face sitting across the table might lift the gloom and help take his mind from all that had happened.

Trucks rumbled in the distance. County road vehicles probably laying salt. Main stretch to town should be in decent shape by midmorning. In time for church.

The good reverend would hold services no matter how many folks gathered for worship.

And Tina's funeral?

The loss cut through him again.

Wade had insisted on holding the service tomorrow. But Nolan agreed with his houseguest. A bit too —

"Dinner smells delicious."

He turned at the sound of Kate's voice.

She stood in the doorway to the kitchen, crutches propped under her arms. Her hair was piled on top of her head, stray tendrils falling around her cheeks.

Still pale, she wore the sky-blue sweatpants and jacket he and Heather had bought at the local clothing store and looked like a teddy bear that needed a hug.

And a good meal. The velour hung on her slender frame.

"Let me help you." He pulled a chair from the table and stepped toward her.

"I've been practicing in my room. Finally got the hang of it." She hobbled forward, holding her left leg off the floor.

He touched her shoulder, the velour soft in his hand. "I'll take these." He grabbed the crutches and eased her into the chair. Once she was seated, he propped her injured leg on a footstool.

"How's that?"

She grimaced as he scooted her closer to the table. "If I ignore my left side, I'm in good shape."

"Would another ice bag help?"

She rubbed her injured leg. "Probably not, Nolan. But thanks. Just give me a minute."

"I've got herbal tea brewing for Heather. How about a cup?"

Kate glanced at the pot on the counter and nodded. "Sure, that sounds good."

He wiped his hands on his pants, suddenly at odds with what to do next.

Think, Price. Pour the tea. Stir the sauce. Cook the spaghetti.

Her eyes looked questioningly up at him. Big blue eyes edged with apprehension.

It must be disconcerting to have her life put on hold. And in Mercy, Georgia, of all places. He could appreciate her concern.

"Seems strange not to have Tina scurrying around the kitchen. South of the border was her specialty. Enchiladas, burritos, guacamole." He noticed the moisture pooling in Kate's eyes. "Look, I've upset you."

She shook her head and sniffed. "I'm fine, really."

He poured the tea and handed her a cup. "You and Tina were next-door neighbors in El Paso. If you don't mind my asking, what brought you to Georgia?"

"It was purely economics. I'm a chemist and needed a job. A spot opened at Ban-

70

nister Scientific about six months ago. Luckily, I landed the position."

"Chemist, huh? Don't know if you realized, but Lloyd seemed rather taken aback by your scientific expertise."

"I noticed he doesn't like his authority questioned."

"Exactly."

"And your line of work?" she asked.

"Basically, I help companies with their investment decisions. Mergers, consolidations, global expansion, that type of thing."

"You're a financial analyst?"

"That's right." Nolan stirred the pasta into the boiling water, thinking back to what he'd read about Bannister Scientific. "Wasn't there something in the paper recently about that company of yours?"

Kate nodded. "Unfortunately, yes. The reporter did a bit of embellishing. Amazing how a quote can change after a little cut and paste."

"Now I remember. The article had to do with transplants. That's not what you're working on, is it?"

"Matter of fact, it is."

The back of Nolan's neck prickled. "What — what type of transplants are you researching?"

"Pancreatic cells involved in insulin pro-

71

duction. My grandfather was a diabetic, and
—"

Nolan exhaled the breath he'd been holding. "Let me guess. Because of him you went into research?"

She tilted her head and smiled. "That's right."

"Made your parents proud, no doubt."

Kate started to reply, then appeared to reconsider. She pulled the cup to her lips and took another sip.

Had he said something wrong? "Look, I —"

Water boiled over the edge of the pot and hissed as it hit the hot burner below. Nolan yanked the pot from the flame at the same moment the door to the hallway opened.

Heather stepped into the kitchen and glanced from Kate to her father. "Sorry to interrupt."

"Dinner's almost ready, hon."

His daughter grabbed a mug from the cabinet and poured tea into the cup as he drained the pasta into the colander in the sink. Steam rose in the air.

"I'm not hungry, Dad."

Before he could respond, she turned on her heel and left the room.

"Heather?" Nolan called after her.

No response.

Seemed he was batting zero for two.

He'd struck out with his daughter, and from the look on Kate's face, she probably wished she'd chosen another ballpark.

Not a good night for the home team.

And they were only in the first inning.

FIVE

A wave of raw emotion washed over Nolan's face. He placed the empty pot back on the stove, raised his hands in the air and let out a deep sigh. "I don't know what to do. After Olivia died, my daughter . . ."

He looked at Kate, pain and worry reflected in his eyes. "I didn't know if she'd make it. Olivia's death rocked us both, but Heather . . ." He shook his head. "Took her a long time to heal. Now with Tina gone —"

"Why don't you talk to her," Kate encouraged. "I'll watch the stove."

"You wouldn't mind?" He seemed genuinely appreciative.

"Go." She pointed to the door.

"Thanks." He hurried into the hallway. The stairs creaked as he climbed to the second floor.

Heather was trying to be strong, the effort taking a toll. All that hurt had to surface.

74

No doubt, her withdrawal was in response to her pain.

The girl probably needed to cry her eyes out on her dad's broad shoulders. Something Nolan failed to realize.

Men could be so clueless. Kate knew too well. Her own dad had turned his back on her need more times than she cared to remember. She'd finally shut down the pain, buried it deep within her. Maybe not deep enough.

Bracing herself on one crutch, Kate hobbled to the stove and stirred the thick tomato sauce. Her stomach rumbled. Good old Pavlovian response to the rich aroma swirling around her.

She opened a couple drawers until she found a teaspoon, dipped into the simmering marinara and savored the hearty blend.

Hadn't had sauce that good since she was a girl. She thought back to sitting in her grandfather's kitchen, waiting expectantly as he held a spoon to her lips.

"Careful, Katie-girl, sauce is hot. Don't burn that sweet mouth of yours."

Good ol' Grandda with a big heart and ability to make her feel lovable and loved. Tears stung in her eyes.

"Too spicy?"

Kate whirled around. Nolan stood in the

doorway. She hadn't heard him coming down the stairs.

She forced a laugh. "Spicy, but good."

"Glad you like it." He pulled two plates from the cabinet and placed them on the counter. "I was in a creative mood a few years ago. Ended up with a recipe worth keeping. Been fixing it ever since."

"Sauce reminds me of what my grandfather used to make."

"He liked to cook?"

"And I liked to eat. If he'd lived longer, I'd probably weigh two hundred pounds."

"Nothing compares with a little Italian soul food. Heather usually dives in and doesn't come up for air until she's finished. Tonight . . ." He paused. "I'll take a plate to her after we eat."

Apparently, he hadn't gotten a chance to comfort his daughter. Such a shame. The girl was closing off the person who probably loved her most.

If Kate had the opportunity before she went back to Atlanta, she'd have a chat with the teen. Tell her how lucky she was to have a father who cared. Not that Heather would necessarily listen to a stranger's advice.

"May I set the table?" Kate asked, wanting to help.

"If it's not too much trouble with those

crutches. Silverware's in the top —" He stopped and glanced down at the teaspoon she'd used, then smiled. "Guess you already found the drawer."

She grabbed the utensils and arranged them on the table before she sat down and dropped the crutches on the floor beside her.

Nolan arranged two lit candles in the center of the table, then he filled the plates with spaghetti and ladled the thick sauce on top.

"More tea?" he asked, placing a heaping plate in front of Kate.

"I'm fine."

He slipped into the chair across from her. The flickering candles framed the table in a circle of light as the night settled around them.

Before she could reach for her fork, Kate sensed Nolan's eyes on her. Dropping her hands to her lap, she looked up.

He raised an eyebrow, his mouth firm, a hint of five o'clock shadow darkening the corners of his square jaw. "Shall we give thanks?"

She bowed her head, cheeks burning in proportion to her rising discomfort level. Prayer hadn't been on her menu for years.

She swallowed down the anxiety bubbling

up within her. Taking the next bus to Atlanta seemed like a good idea at the moment. If there was a bus.

"Father, we give You thanks for the blessings of this day," he started to pray.

Blessings? What blessings? Her leg throbbed, she was dead tired and the only lodging in town was with a family almost as dysfunctional as her own had been.

"All around us, Lord, the beauty of Your creation shines forth . . ."

Was Nolan Price living in a dream world? From what Kate had heard last night, Heather blamed him for her mother's death. In addition, his daughter had trouble articulating the gut-wrenching sense of loss Tina's death had caused. As if that wasn't enough, he'd taken in a stray who carried more than her fair share of baggage. Not what Kate would call a good day.

"We see the power of Your mighty majesty in this winter storm . . ."

And he was giving thanks?

Either Nolan Price had his head in the sand or he was just plain stupid.

Someone needed to give the man a reality check.

"Lord, we know You've brought Kate into our lives for a reason . . ."

She jerked her head up. What reason?

". . . Bless us and the food we are about to eat. Amen."

Unnerved, Kate sat for a minute, staring down at her plate, before she reached for the fork.

"Something wrong?" Nolan asked as he started to eat. A line of concern crossed his brow, yet his eyes, bathed in candlelight, were warmly encouraging.

"It's just that . . ." She clenched her left hand in her lap. "You saved my life. Then you opened your home to me. Your hospitality —"

"Kate, you've thanked me already. Say it one more time and I'll get a complex. Like maybe you think I've got a hearing problem. Truth be told, if you weren't here, I'd be eating alone tonight."

He glanced away, pulled in a deep breath. When he looked back at her, the dejection she saw in his eyes tore at her heart. His strong facade had chipped away, exposing — at least for the moment — the depth of his grief.

Suddenly, she wanted to comfort him. "Heather reminds me of myself." The words flew from her mouth before she had a chance to stop them.

"Really?" He tilted his head, a glimmer of hope evident in his eyes.

"I was a . . . well, I guess you'd say, a difficult child. My mom died when I was born. Preeclampsia."

"Pre-what?"

"It's also called toxemia. Occurs in women close to delivery. High blood pressure, protein buildup." She placed the fork on her plate. "Dad didn't have insurance. Seems my mother cut corners by skipping her prenatal care." Kate shrugged. "It all added to the mix."

"I'm sorry."

"Hey, you've had more than your share of problems. Tough to lose your soul mate."

He sighed. "Olivia and I had a good marriage. Then . . ." He straightened in his chair. "Things change. You know what I mean?"

Funny. She did know. All too well. In a split second, as fast as a spark ignited into flames, everything that seemed safe and comfortable and good could be lost.

Not tonight! *I can't think about that tonight.*

"Don't get me wrong," Nolan continued. "It's just that after seventeen years you expect a few bumps in the road, but . . ."

"But not sickness and death."

He dropped his gaze and shook his head. "Never that."

Unsure of how to respond, Kate said

80

nothing and picked at her food until she could no longer ignore the question that gnawed at her. "Answer me one thing, Nolan."

He looked up, his eyes as black as the darkness that swirled outside the candle-light.

For half a heartbeat, she recalled the sensation of him carrying her to safety. *Where had that come from?*

She cleared her throat, willed her voice to carry a light-hearted lilt. "This spaghetti certainly is delicious." Hopefully, he wouldn't notice her abrupt subject change.

He continued to stare at her. "You wanted to ask me a question?"

"Right." *Sometimes you talk too much, Kate Murphy.* She sighed, buying time as she carefully chose her words. "I guess I want to know, after the pain of loss you've suffered —"

He raised an eyebrow. "Yes?"

"How can you still believe in God?"

He looked at her for a long moment before asking, "Would the pain be any less if I *didn't* believe in Him?"

"I . . . I'm not sure."

"What about you, Kate? Are you a believer?"

"I was. Then . . ." She glanced into the

darkness. Too much had happened. "It's not so much that I don't believe in God. It's that I don't believe He loves *me*."

"He loves all His children."

She nodded. "Children, yes. Twenty-nine-year-old women who have made a mess of their lives, I'm not so sure about."

"Funny, Tina said almost those very same words."

A lump formed in Kate's throat as Nolan continued. "Tina's life changed once she realized God's forgiveness and mercy were unconditional, just like His love."

"That sounds too easy."

"Have you prayed, Kate?"

Her right hand reached for her neck, seeking strength from Grandda's gold cross. But she'd given it to Eddie. Along with her heart.

Pray? Sure, she'd prayed. When her grandfather's glucose had gone sky high, she'd asked the Lord to intervene.

Just as she had that night at the cabin.

But her grandfather had died, then two months later, Eddie had gone into his maniacal tirade. Easy to piece the rest together. An overturned table, a smoldering candle fanned into flames and the chemicals Eddie had stolen from her university lab had gone up with a bang.

"Yes, I prayed. But in my opinion, God practices selective hearing."

"Then I'll pray for you."

"Don't do me any favors, Nolan. As far as I'm concerned —"

The overhead light snapped on, catching her midsentence. They both blinked against the sudden brightness.

"Modern conveniences back in working mode," Nolan said.

For an instant, Kate yearned for the darkness. The glare of light exposed every flaw. Better not to see the less-than-perfect details.

"My leg's hurting. If you don't mind, Nolan, I'd like to go to my room."

Worry lines creased the corners of his eyes. Kate hadn't noticed them in the candlelight.

She picked up her crutches, scooted her chair back and pushed herself up.

Rounding the table, Nolan took Kate's arm and guided her toward the hallway. "Heather and I will leave for church a little before eleven in the morning. If you feel up to it —"

Kate shook her head. "No. But Tina's funeral." She hesitated, swallowed. "I'd like to go."

"Of course. I'll get the exact time in the

morning." Nolan stopped at the door to her room. "Thanks for your encouragement about Heather."

"Your daughter's a beautiful girl, Nolan. She just needs a little time and a lot of love."

He stood there for a moment. His eyes bored into her.

Had he heard what she said? "You understand, don't you, Nolan? Heather needs love to heal."

"Good advice, Kate. Why don't you follow it yourself?"

"What?"

"Allow God's love into your heart. He'll help you heal."

She didn't want or need Nolan's advice. She'd tried the God route before. Didn't work.

"Good night, Nolan." Kate stepped into the bedroom and closed the door.

The guy had it all wrong. Nolan had the problem, not her. She wasn't the one who had closed her heart.

Or was she?

Maybe they were both fighting the same demons.

Nolan left Kate at the door to the guest room and headed for the basement. What would cause a woman to turn her back on God?

He shook his head as he hastened down the stairs.

A lot of pain. He could see it in her eyes.

Oh, yeah, he was an expert when it came to pain. Olivia's trip, her surgery, the infection that took her life. Now Tina. He pulled in a deep breath. On top of everything, he and Heather were on rocky ground. He loved his daughter more than anyone would ever know. She gave meaning to his life, gave him a reason to go on.

After his wife's death, he could hardly draw a breath without a sharp jab of grief and guilt cutting his heart in two. He'd forced himself to move forward for Heather's sake, maintaining some sense of normalcy for the good of his child.

Not that Heather had noticed. She'd hung a Keep Out sign on the door to her heart and started a slow, deliberate process of excluding him.

He didn't need Kate to remind him they could use some work in the relationship department. Besides, his drive-by boarder had enough problems of her own.

It had to be troubling to recuperate in a strange home far from Atlanta. Although Kate didn't appear eager to let anyone know about her accident. Surely, she'd want to contact a girlfriend or a colleague at work?

He stepped into his basement office and closed the door behind him.

Even if Kate didn't have anyone to call, he did.

Relieved the cell towers were up and running at long last, Nolan dropped into the leather desk chair, picked up his cell and tapped in the long-distance number.

Nice to be connected to the rest of the world again.

He checked his watch and did the math. Five forty-five in Georgia. Three hours earlier in California.

Dave Reynolds was probably heading down the fairway on the back nine. Fortunately, he kept his cell phone on 24/7.

A deep baritone answered the third ring. "Reynolds."

"How's my good friend and favorite private investigator?"

"Enjoying life on your buck."

Nolan sat back in his chair. "My guess, you're three under par and just two-putted for a birdie."

Dave laughed, a deep rumble that echoed over the line. "Seventy degrees, clear skies. Perfect golf weather, my man. Unfortunately, I'm following the trail of a dirtbag husband who keeps forgetting he needs to pay child support. Mama and five little ones at home and the guy skates."

"Let me guess. You're working pro bono?"

"And charging my high-end clients, like you, double."

Nolan chuckled. "What are friends for?"

"From what the weatherman said, you must be bundled up for a deep freeze."

"Ice storm. We lost power and phone connections in the night. The cell towers were affected, as well. My phone just came back on or I would have called you earlier."

"What's up?"

Nolan raked his hand through his hair and sighed. "Another accident victim."

"What's that make? Five in two months?"

"This one hit home."

"Meaning . . . ?"

"Meaning the dead-on-arrival was my housekeeper."

Dave cursed.

A lump formed in Nolan's throat. Had his quest for justice cost Tina her life?

Lord, help me.

"Nolan, I'm so sorry, man."

"The town G.P. claimed Tina had an allergic reaction to latex. Went into anaphylactic shock. She died yesterday."

"But . . ." Dave hesitated. "As they say in

the South, you don't cotton to the doc, now do you?"

"I told you about his middle-of-the-night escapades."

"Roger that. And as I recall, you never told the housekeeper the real reason you moved to Mercy."

Nolan sighed. "In hindsight, it was probably a mistake on my part. Her service is tomorrow. Too fast, in my opinion, but the funeral director claimed Sunday interment is common in these parts."

"And you believe him?"

"About as much as I believe the doc."

"Could Tina's death be a warning?"

The hairs on Nolan's neck tingled. "To back off?"

"Exactly. Maybe they realized you were a little too interested in the doctor's business."

Nolan shook his head. "Far as anyone knows, I'm a financial analyst who wanted to move my teenage daughter out of L.A."

"You're sure Olivia used an alias while she was in Mercy?"

"And paid for the treatment in cash. No paper trail. No way they'd connect me with a transplant tourist they saw eight months ago."

"Could Heather have told one of the kids

at school?"

"About her mother?"

Dave sighed with exasperation. "That's the issue, isn't it?"

Nolan flicked a speck of dust off his mahogany desk. "If anyone asks, she says her mother died of an infection."

"Yeah, but one slip of the tongue. Maybe to a boyfriend."

Nolan thought of Jimmy and bristled. "She's too young to date."

"Uh-huh. Get real, Dad. Girls like boys, boys like girls, even if you think she's not old enough."

"Dave —"

"Look, Nolan, I may be working for you, but I'm your friend first. Remember that long talk we had? I told you to stay put in L.A."

"And what was I supposed to do? Twiddle my thumbs while the police did nothing?"

"Caution's the name of the game when high-profile types are involved."

Nolan gave a disgusted laugh. "You mean people who fund campaign coffers? People like Sanjeer Hira?"

"The clinical director's well connected, but they searched the Beverly Hills Specialty Clinic and found nothing illegal. Every *t* was crossed. Every *i* dotted."

"Paperwork can be forged to look legit. Medical records can be falsified, Dave." Nolan rubbed the back of his neck. "That's why I *had* to come to Mercy. If I can gather enough evidence on this small-time operation in rural Georgia, I may be able to link them to Hira."

"Last thing I should do is encourage you, but I have some news on this end. I made a new contact. A cute little LPN. Likes to talk, especially after her evening shift at the Beverly Hills Specialty Center. We've grown pretty chummy."

"Keep it aboveboard. Understand, Dave?"

"Hey, I'm a nice guy. She calls me a teddy bear."

"Yeah, right." Six foot and all muscle. Nothing cute and cuddly about Dave. "Has she given you any information yet?"

"Only that a wealthy Hollywood type is seeking Dr. Hira's medical expertise after hours."

"Maybe we'll get lucky."

"Everything takes time, Nolan."

"Which I don't have. I want this whole thing wrapped up tight so Heather —"

"So Heather will stop blaming you for what happened to her mother. You're still racked with guilt, aren't you?"

"Of course I am. I feel responsible. If we'd

90

had a better marriage —"

"You don't have to earn your daughter's love, Nolan. She'll come around whether you catch the bad guys or not. But this one-man crusade you're on has me worried. Get out while you can."

"Trust me, Dave. I won't be here much longer. But there's something else I'd like you to look into."

"Shoot."

"An old friend of Tina's dropped into town. Evidently, they grew up together. El Paso. Near the border. Tina's family was dirt poor. Conditions were pretty bleak. Seems this friend managed to get herself a college degree. Her name's Kate Murphy. She works at Bannister Scientific, a research lab in Atlanta."

"Interesting. You think she's involved?"

"No way. I just —" Nolan sighed. Why *did* he want Dave to look into Kate's background? Probably because she'd said she'd made a mess of her life and turned her back on God. If Nolan knew what had happened, he might be able to help.

"Just see what you can find out. I thought since she knew Tina . . . well, I wanted to learn a little more about her. She had a car accident on the way here and she's recuperating in our guest room."

"Could be a wolf in sheep's clothing."

Interesting for Dave to use the same phrase Nolan had read in scripture earlier. "More like a lost soul. Let me know what you uncover."

"Roger that, *mi amigo.* Watch your back."

Nolan would do more than watch his back; he'd uncover the truth about what was happening in Mercy.

And Kate Murphy?

Maybe he could help her, as well.

Six

Kate woke Sunday morning to a full body ache. Wincing as her stiff muscles protested, she took a hot shower, then slipped into another of Nolan's purchases — a sweatshirt and baggy pants that fit over her brace. Grabbing the crutches, she opened the door to her room and followed the smell of perked coffee to the kitchen.

Nolan stood at the counter, wearing a white dress shirt, open at the collar, and dark slacks. He turned as she entered; a hint of sunlight filtered through the window behind him as welcoming as his smile.

"You look rested," he said.

"I slept well, thanks. Any chance you've got an extra cup of coffee?" She dropped her crutches to the floor and slid into a chair at the table.

Nolan poured the rich-smelling brew and handed her the mug. "How's the leg?"

"I'm ignoring it, hoping it'll go away."

"Gotcha. Can I fix you breakfast before Heather and I leave for church? Bacon and eggs?"

"Maybe a little juice."

"English muffin? It's whole wheat."

He certainly liked to push food. "Thank you, Nolan. A muffin would be great."

Kate took a sip of her coffee and watched him drop the two muffin sections into the toaster. "If you don't mind my asking, where'd you learn to cook?"

He glanced at her over his shoulder and shrugged. "Mainly trial and error. Heather forced the issue. When a little one's hungry, a guy can learn real fast."

What about the guy's wife? "So you were Mr. Mom?"

"Of sorts. Olivia was getting her degree, filming documentaries on the side." He turned to face Kate. "Not much time left in a day."

"Documentaries?"

"Social justice pieces," he explained. "Mothers on welfare, migrant farmers, teenage prostitution. Olivia fought for the underdog, the oppressed. Shooting schedules sometimes overlapped with dinner, so I started to fill in."

Kate sipped her coffee as he poured

orange juice and placed the glass on the table.

"Found I enjoyed the creative part of cooking," Nolan continued. "Throw a few ingredients into a pot. See how it turns out. Know what I mean?"

Kate laughed. "Not really. My idea of gourmet is Lean Cuisine and a bag of pre-washed arugula."

The toaster popped. Nolan dropped the muffin onto a plate and placed it in front of her along with butter and jelly.

"See, you're spoiling me." She laughed.

"Aim to please, ma'am." He feigned a Texas twang and tipped an imaginary hat before he dug a hand into his right pants pocket and pulled out a cell. "Phone started working last night. Thought you might want to call someone. Let them know about your wreck." He placed the cell on the table. "Unlimited long distance. Talk as long as you want."

The man thought of everything. "Thank you, Nolan."

"Well . . ." He shuffled his feet. "I need to finish getting ready for church."

She buttered her muffin as he left the room. His footsteps echoed in the hallway, then climbed the stairs to the second floor.

"Heather, honey. Almost ready?" The

words drifted down the stairs.

A phone rang somewhere in the house.

Kate glanced down at the silent cell.

Who could she call? Jason Bannister was out of town for a three-day weekend. His secretary wouldn't be back at her desk until Monday morning. No one else at the lab needed to know about Kate's predicament.

Relatives? An elderly uncle on her mother's side. Long-term Alzheimer's. He'd forgotten Kate's name a year ago.

Most times the reality of not having family didn't affect her. Today was an exception. Sitting in Nolan's cozy kitchen brought back memories of her grandfather's home and the love she'd felt from the man who had taken her in when her father had wanted nothing to do with her.

She heard Nolan retrace his steps. As he walked into the room, Kate wished she'd done more than brush her hair this morning.

Sporting a red tie and navy jacket, he looked like a slick magazine advertisement, all chiseled angles and rugged good looks.

She swallowed, a bite of muffin lodging in her throat. Reaching for the juice, she gulped a long swig. He certainly had an effect on her composure.

"You okay?" he asked.

She nodded, swallowed again and hoped her voice would work. "How're the roads?"

Stupid question. One peek outside and any idiot would know they were still slick and treacherous.

"Trucks dumped salt all night. Shouldn't be a problem. The undertaker called a minute ago. Tina's funeral will follow the morning service. I'll swing by and get you after church."

She glanced down at the sweatshirt and pants. "Didn't the nurse give me a bag with my wet clothing?"

"That's right. The outfit you were wearing the night of the crash. I'll take it to the cleaners tomorrow. In the meantime, I asked Heather if she had anything you could wear."

The thought of trying to stuff her twenty-nine-year-old body into a trendy teenage outfit made her want to stay put. She'd feel more comfortable mourning here at the house. "You go without me."

"Nonsense." He stepped into the foyer and called, "Heather. Time for church."

The teen's labored steps slowly descended to the first floor. She entered the kitchen dressed in a dark green skirt and red sweater, looking like a Christmas elf with a bah-humbug attitude.

"Dad said you needed something to wear." Heather dropped a bundle of clothing on the table. "I tried to find something that was . . ." She looked at Kate, then back at her dad. "Well, something for an *older* woman."

Kate had to bite her lip to keep from smiling. She certainly didn't think of herself as old. "It's very kind of you."

The girl flipped her hair over her shoulder. "Sure, no problem. Dad told me you and Tina were friends. She'd want you at her funeral."

"Thank you, Heather."

"We'll be back in an hour," Nolan said to Kate as he nudged his daughter out the door. The rumble of a garage opening and the sputter of a car engine sounded through the cold morning air.

Kate clutched the mug even tighter, appreciating the warmth as the sound of the car faded into the distance. The house seemed too quiet without Nolan hovering about the kitchen.

Finishing the coffee and bracing the crutches under her arms, Kate gathered the clothing, shuffled into her room and locked the door behind her.

" 'Fraidy cat, 'fraidy cat," she mumbled, recalling the taunt the boys on the playground had chanted long ago.

She'd never been the bravest kid on the block. Her grandfather had called it a fear of abandonment. She didn't like to be alone.

Shaking off the thought, Kate unfolded the dress Heather had given her. Not something she would have chosen but appropriate for a funeral.

Heather had included a pair of black flats, nylon stockings and a short wool jacket.

No hope fitting the nylons over her injured leg. Kate backtracked to the bathroom, unwrapped a travel sewing kit and used the scissors to cut off one of the legs. Ten minutes later, she glanced in the mirror. The knit dress accentuated her slender shape more than she would have liked, but at least it fit.

With her good leg sporting the nylon stocking and the other strapped in the immobilizer, Kate grabbed her crutches and hobbled back to the kitchen. Nolan had offered his cell phone for her to call a friend and though that wasn't necessary, she should notify her insurance company.

Kate plugged in the number and waited as a mechanical recording guided her through a series of prompts. "Auto claims, press two."

She tapped the digit.

"This call may be recorded for quality assurance. Please stand by. The next available clerk will assist you shortly."

Drumming her fingers on the table, Kate watched the minutes tick by on the wall clock. Calling on a Sunday had probably been a mistake.

Just as she was ready to snap the phone shut, an operator answered, accessed her file and twenty minutes later assured her that damages — less her deductible — would be covered.

With a sigh of relief, Kate lowered the phone and pushed the disconnect button. Her hand slipped, knocking it from the table.

She lunged to catch the elusive cell. Her fingers closed around the digit pad as a jolt of fire sliced through her leg.

"Ahhhh!" She fisted her hands and fought back with deep breaths until the pain subsided.

Relaxing her grip, she raised the phone to her ear to ensure the call had ended.

"You have one voice mail. Friday, 1:15 p.m."

What? Nolan's voice mail? How'd that happen?

Before she could snap the phone shut, she heard Tina's voice.

"Nolan. I've got to talk to you," the recorded message said. "I saw something —"

A key turned in the back door.

Kate yanked the cell from her ear just as Nolan opened the door. He looked first at Kate, then at the cell in her hand before he stamped his feet on the entry mat and closed the door hard behind him.

Kate's cheeks burned. She placed the cell on the table. "I called my insurance company."

"Everything okay?"

"Fine."

Tina had said she didn't know whom to trust when she had talked to Kate at one o'clock Friday afternoon. Fifteen minutes later, Tina had left the message for Nolan.

"Ready?" Nolan grabbed the jacket from the chair and slipped it over Kate's shoulders.

No. She wasn't ready.

Kate wanted to scoot into the guest room, lock the door behind her and wait until someone from Atlanta could drive her back to the sanity her life had been.

But she needed to learn what Tina had seen in the woods and whether it had something to do with her death.

SEVEN

Nolan drove along the country road, relieved the salt had melted most of the ice. Although the heater was set on high, the temperature in the car seemed as chilly as the winter scene rolling past the windows.

Heather sat next to him in the passenger seat, totally absorbed in picking polish off her nails. Kate had slipped into the rear, propped her injured leg across the bench seat and stared out the window as if the ice-laden pine trees were more interesting than the people inside the car.

Nolan's attempts at conversation had fallen flat. The silence began to wear on him. Ever since he'd stepped into the kitchen and seen Kate again, he'd reacted as if he'd taken a hard left jab and had the air knocked out of his lungs. It was even easier to see how pretty Kate was when she'd put some care into her appearance. His reaction surprised him.

He stole another glance at his rear-seat passenger. Cat had her tongue. Last night, she'd been a chatterbox.

Why's it bug you, Price? He had a mission to accomplish, and it didn't involve getting close to another woman.

Doubtful Kate wanted anything to do with him, either. From the looks of things, she had closed herself off as tightly as Heather had.

Women! They were becoming more of an enigma every day. At least Olivia had been straightforward. Maybe too much so. No dancing around an issue or mixed signals with confusing double talk. She knew what she wanted and had gone after it. Three small documentaries and she'd had Hollywood taking notice.

He'd been a fool to think her work with the underprivileged would be enough. When she'd told him she wanted more, he hadn't believed her.

Maybe because he'd thought they were cut from the same cloth, both determined to make a difference in the world. In his mind that meant following the Gospel message — feed the hungry, shelter the homeless, visit the sick.

At first, Olivia had been committed to helping others. Then the secular world had come to call and her priorities had changed. In hindsight, Nolan realized she'd been biding her time, gathering momentum to break into the limelight at the most opportune moment.

Fame, adulation, success. Olivia thrived on it, while Nolan had stood in the wings, trying to hold their marriage together.

He glanced at Heather. Everyone said the teenage years were tough. Compound that with Olivia's death and a move cross-country. He'd known changing the Hollywood glitz for rural Georgia would be hard on his daughter. He hadn't realized how hard.

As soon as he had the evidence he needed, they'd move someplace safe. Somewhere he and Heather could rediscover what it meant to be a family — a family of two.

Nolan eased the car around the bend in the road. The church came into view. He turned into the parking lot just as Doc Samuels stepped outside, raised a hand in greeting, then walked toward the car.

"Afternoon, Kate," he said as he opened the rear door for her. "How's the leg?"

She grabbed the crutches. "Better. I'm getting around by myself."

The doctor searched her face. "Taking those pain pills I prescribed?"

"Of course."

"Drowsy?"

Kate glanced at Nolan as he stepped from the car. "A little."

Not that Nolan had noticed. Today, she seemed alert and focused.

The doc took Kate's arm and steadied her as she hobbled toward the church.

Wade Green stepped outside and shook Nolan's hand. Five-ten, twenty pounds overweight and marked with a perpetual frown, Wade appeared as lifeless as the bodies he buried.

"Reverend Ames is almost ready to start the service. You folks sit up front." The funeral director turned to Kate. "I heard you knew Tina."

"We were old friends."

Wade nodded. "I'm very sorry for your loss."

Kate blinked, opened her mouth as if to say something, then pulled in a deep breath. "Thank you," she finally mumbled as she inched her way inside.

Nolan's heart weighed heavily. He still couldn't believe Tina was dead. If only they could backtrack a week. He'd give anything to have Tina walking next to Heather into the sanctuary to worship instead of the reality of today.

Guilt pricked him.

He didn't want to think he was responsible, but he had to wonder. Had his need to follow this trail to Mercy led to Tina's death?

Kate felt the eyes of the congregation staring at her as Nolan placed his hand on the small of her back and guided her into the front left pew usually reserved for the deceased's family.

Not where Kate wanted to sit.

Heather slid in next to her, and Nolan took the seat on the end.

Organ chords filled the sanctuary. Somber music in keeping with the occasion. An open Bible and a small urn sat on a table centered in front of the wooden altar.

Tina's ashes.

A lump formed in Kate's throat.

The organist leaned into her microphone. "Turn to hymn seventy-seven in your songbooks."

The congregation stood. Kate stared straight ahead. Singing was more than she could manage.

Heather slumped next to her, the girl's eyes downcast as she examined her nails. At the end of the pew, Nolan's rich baritone sounded above the other voices.

Tina dead. Along with Eddie and Mrs. Espinosa. Kate sucked in a deep breath and bit down on her lower lip, trying to focus on something other than three deaths in three years.

And it had all started that night at the cabin.

After all she and Eddie had shared.

She'd believed him when he'd told her she was special . . . that they would always be together . . . that he'd do anything for her.

Empty promises to gain access to her university lab and the chemicals she researched.

Naive. And blinded by love. She hadn't connected the missing inventory with Eddie's visits.

Not until everything had come together the night she'd thought he would ask her to marry him. The night he'd tried to force himself on her. The night she'd run for her life.

The memory made her stomach roil and her cheeks burn. She'd been such a fool!

The minister stepped to the pulpit as the last chords of the hymn faded and the congregation settled into their seats. "Dearly beloved, we have come here today to ask God's blessings on the soul of our sister in

Christ, Tina Espinosa."

Kate's chest ached. Sister in Christ?

When had Tina given her heart to God?

Three years ago, she'd been filled with anything but the love of the Lord. Wrapped up in her brother's fiery death, Tina had refused to listen to the truth and called Kate a liar.

Eddie's illegal attempt to feed his addiction had been more than Tina could bear. She hadn't liked the message, so she'd turned her back on the messenger.

Not the saint the reverend thought he knew.

". . . and into Your hands, Lord, we commend her spirit." The preacher paused as the congregation waited with expectation. "Nolan Price has asked to say a few words."

Someone coughed and others sighed before a notable quiet settled over the church. Nolan stepped to the pulpit and nodded to the minister.

"Thank you, Reverend." His eyes flicked over the crowd. "It is with deep sorrow that I stand before you today."

Heather hung her head. Kate glanced at the child. The pain she saw tore Kate in two.

"Tina was more than an employee," Nolan began. "She was like a member of our family. In the short time since we moved to

Mercy, Tina had become an important member of this church family, as well."

A tear ran down Heather's face. She scrubbed her hand over her cheek, clenched her lips and struggled for control.

"You all know what a caring person Tina was and the good she did." Nolan's voice resounded in the sanctuary. "The Lord walked with Tina in life. He walks with her in death, as well."

Heather's dam of self-control broke. A flood of tears cascaded down her pain-twisted face.

Without a moment's hesitation, Kate pulled the girl into her arms and held her tightly against her heart.

Heather folded into her embrace. Like a drowning victim tossed on tumultuous seas, Heather held on for dear life.

Nolan's eyes locked on Kate's. "We . . . We all benefited from Tina's outreach."

Kate pulled away from his gaze and buried her face in the girl's thick mane of hair, smelling the peach scent of her shampoo, feeling the warmth of her body, the thump, thump, thump of her heart beating in sync with Kate's.

Heather's need touched a spot deep inside Kate. "Shh," she soothed.

Tina and Kate had been inseparable,

kindred spirits. That was why it had hurt so much when Tina had cut Kate out of her life.

Now Tina's death had sliced a hole in Heather's heart, as well. Without a doubt, the child felt the knife-sharp pain just as surely as Kate had three years ago.

But Heather was young and still reeling from her mother's death.

Kate glanced up at the stark wooden cross hanging behind the altar. Why would a loving God give this child such a heavy burden without sending someone to help carry her load?

Life wasn't fair. Kate knew that all too well.

Tears stung her eyes. She blinked, forcing the memories into the deep recesses of her heart.

Nolan's face swam into view. He was staring down at her. His eyes were dark pools of compassion that pierced her broken exterior as if he could see into her soul.

If he looked deep enough, what would he find?

A woman searching for love.

The thought tore through her mind. She glanced away, not willing to let Nolan see the truth written on her heart.

Gently, she rocked Heather in her arms as

Nolan's voice continued to fill the sanctuary. At the conclusion of the eulogy, he stepped from the pulpit, and the minister called the congregation to prayer. Slipping into the pew, Nolan stared at Kate, brow wrinkled, worry etched on his face.

"She's okay," Kate mouthed, clutching the child even more tightly to her chest. Heather's tears eased, but she remained wrapped in Kate's arms for the remainder of the service.

After the final hymn, the reverend invited the congregation into the hall for lunch. As the sanctuary cleared, Heather reached for the tissue Kate offered. The girl blew her nose and wiped her face dry, then straightened her shoulders and sighed deeply before she glanced at Kate. Her lip quivered into a partial smile. "I got your dress wet."

Kate smiled back. "It's your dress, remember? Won't hurt a thing."

The girl picked at the tissue in her hand. "Sorry I cried through your talk, Dad."

Nolan stroked her arm. "We all grieve in different ways, honey. When you're ready, we'll head into the hall and get something to eat."

She nodded. "Let me run to the restroom first. My face is all yucky."

"You look beautiful, hon."

Kate would have given anything for her own father to tell her she was beautiful. Seemed a ray of light had broken through their loss.

Heather left the sanctuary, leaving Nolan to accompany Kate into the hall where Reverend Ames greeted them at the door.

"Tina would have appreciated an old friend in the congregation today," he said to Kate. "Hope you'll join us for worship next Sunday."

"I'll be back home in Atlanta by then, but thank you for the invitation, Reverend."

A long buffet table lined with hot casseroles and chilled salads, rolls and desserts stretched across one side of the room. Nolan ushered Kate forward. She grabbed a plate and started through the line.

"Let me have that," he said, seeing her struggle with her crutches. "Find a seat, and I'll bring the food to you. What's your preference?"

"Anything will be fine. Thanks."

Kate headed for an oblong table where a gray-haired lady flashed a wide smile and waved a greeting.

"Mind if I join you?" Kate asked, slipping into a chair across from the woman whose wrinkled face scrunched into another grin.

"I was hoping I'd get to meet you. Someone told me Nolan had a houseguest, although I can't remember who. Aren't you a friend of Tina's?"

News traveled fast in Mercy.

The older woman shook her head and tsked. "Terrible, terrible shame. Tina being so young and all. Hate to see life cut short. So painful, don't you know?"

Kate did know about the pain part.

"She was such a sweet thing," the woman continued. "Always helping out. Meals to shut-ins, carrying someone to the doctor when they didn't have a ride. Doing the Lord's work wherever she could. 'Spect I'm not telling you anything new."

"Tina had a way with people," Kate admitted truthfully.

The woman raised a questioning brow. "Honey, what'd you say your name was?"

"Kate Murphy."

"I'm terrible with names. Guess it's my age. By the way, I'm Agnes Heartwell. Pleased to meet you. You'll probably be staying in town a while from the looks of that leg of yours."

"Just another day or two."

"Good to see you, Ms. Agnes." Nolan stepped forward, placed two heaping plates of food on the table and dropped into a chair next to Kate. "How's Sue Ann?"

113

"Dr. Samuels put her on a new antibiotic for that upper respiratory infection she always gets this time of year."

Nolan bowed his head for a moment before he picked up his fork.

"Sue Ann's a paraplegic," Agnes explained to Kate. "Auto accident happened . . . What was it?" The woman rolled her eyes. "Five? Six? No. Must be seven years. Happened on Sue Ann's thirty-second birthday. My husband drove Sue Ann over to Summerton to pick out a birthday gift. Teenage driver ran a red light. Hit the passenger side head-on." Agnes's eyes clouded. "You know kids. Never think their recklessness will hurt someone else. Nearly killed my husband, Harlan, him being behind the wheel and all. He couldn't forgive himself."

Nolan reached across the table and patted the old woman's hand. "Sue Ann's lucky to have you to take care of her."

"Why, I'd do anything —" A look of determination washed over the woman's face. "*Anything* for my baby girl."

"Of course you would. Sue Ann knows that," Nolan assured her.

"I hope so. Although sometimes, when she's having a bad spell, she says some of the most hurtful things. Tells me to find a good nursing home for her. I know Sue

Ann's just thinking about *me,* not wanting to be a burden and all." Agnes shook her head. "As if a child could ever be a burden."

The sincerity of the woman's words touched Kate.

"Ms. Agnes, didn't you say your husband was born and raised in Mercy?" Nolan asked.

Agnes's face brightened. "That's right. The only time Harlan left this area was to go to medical school. That's where we met. Moved back after he got his M.D. Harlan was the town's sole physician until Doc Samuels showed up."

Agnes scooped up a forkful of chicken-and-rice casserole. "Harlan passed away a little under two years ago," she told Kate. "Or was it three? At any rate, Lloyd was here. Meant a lot to the townsfolk to have a second physician close at hand."

"Agnes and Sue Ann live in a large home that sits atop Mercy Mountain," Nolan said. "Overlooks Wade's acreage, Wayne Turner's place, the Hawkins farm."

The Hawkins farm? Where Tina's body had been found.

Agnes fiddled with her fork before raising somber eyes to look at Kate. "Sure, I've got lots of land, but with Harlan gone and Sue Ann needing constant care . . . well, it's been hard, especially with my memory failing like it is. 'Course, I've hired help. And Tina was so good to visit." She shook her head, a melancholy smile on her lips. "My, my, but Sue Ann's gonna miss Tina. Not that the whole town won't feel the loss."

Agnes leaned across the table toward Nolan. "Edith Turner's helping me full-time with Sue Ann and even spent the night Friday."

Agnes caught Kate's eye and pointed her fork at a stocky, middle-aged woman with short hair and a down-turned mouth, sitting at a table on the opposite side of the hall.

"Edith is Sheriff Turner's wife. She's next to Janelle Green. Janelle runs the travel agency and is married to the funeral director. Across the table from them are Ray Forbes and his wife, Sherry. Ray manages the garage in town where your car's being worked on."

Kate glanced across the room. Janelle Green, a pretty woman with long blond hair and dressed in a stylish black suit, smiled back. Edith Turner acknowledged Kate with a nod.

"Edith's a jewel," Agnes continued. "She nursed in a big spinal cord–injury rehab center before she and the sheriff married, so she knows how to handle Sue Ann."

Edith looked like a no-nonsense type of person, and Kate's heart went out to Sue Ann who had to be, as Agnes said, *handled.*

Dr. Samuels rose from his chair next to the funeral director's wife and checked the beeper attached to his belt. With a perfunctory nod to the folks sitting around him, he headed to the door, just as it opened.

"Well, look there." Agnes was watching the door. "Isn't that the Ramos boy walking in with Heather?"

Nolan jerked his head up as the twosome entered the hall.

A little taller than Heather, the boy wore baggy jeans and a knit shirt, his olive skin and dark hair a sharp contrast to Heather's fair complexion.

Nolan placed his fork on his plate and stood. "Excuse me, ladies."

Agnes watched him stride toward the twosome. "Poor Heather. Nolan's so protective. 'Course, Tracy Farrington says his heart's in the right place."

"Who's Tracy?"

Agnes pointed her fork toward a very pregnant woman standing by the dessert cart. The redhead waved back.

"Tracy's due in a couple weeks." Agnes lowered her voice. "No one knows who the father is. Nolan's helping her financially. Probably feels it's his Christian duty."

Christian duty?

The pregnant woman lumbered to the table. "How are you, Aggie?"

"Fine, dear. Have you met Kate Smith?"

"Murphy," Kate gently corrected.

Agnes smiled. "That's right. Kate Murphy. She's staying with Nolan."

Tracy greeted Kate with a sincere smile. "Pleased to meet you. Wish it were under better circumstances."

"Nolan asked Tracy to take over Tina's job," Agnes explained. " 'Course Tracy wasn't planning to move in until after the baby was born."

"I'm sure Heather will love having a little one around," Kate said, her attention torn between the pregnant woman and the center of the hall where Nolan appeared to be laying down the law to Heather and her friend.

Whatever Nolan said caused the boy to turn and head for the door. Heather glared up at her father before she ran off in the opposite direction.

"Tina's death moves the time frame up a bit, doesn't it, Tracy?" Agnes said, pulling Kate back into the conversation. "How in the world did Nolan know he'd need a new housekeeper? He asked you almost a month ago." Agnes shook her head in dismay. "More than a coincidence, if you want my opinion."

From what Nolan had told Kate, he seemed satisfied with Tina's ability and happy about the close relationship she had with Heather. Why would Nolan want a new housekeeper?

"Now, Aggie, you know Nolan's got a heart of gold," Tracy said.

The old woman sniffed. "One would hope."

Kate glanced at Nolan standing alone in the center of the room. Agnes had mentioned Christian duty.

Tina. Tracy. The woman whose family had lost their home in the flood.

Did Nolan reach out to all women in need?

Was that he why he had invited Kate into his home?

Or could there be another reason?

EIGHT

Nolan stepped into his basement office relieved to have Tina's funeral behind him. A hard day for everyone, especially Heather. For so long she'd held her grief inside. Today, she'd finally broken down and cried. A good sign. Yet, her growing attachment to the Ramos boy worried Nolan.

Settling into his desk chair, he let out a ragged breath. At fifteen, Heather thought she was old enough to date a high school junior. What difference did a couple of years make in his daughter's mind?

But Nolan knew teenage boys.

Heather had developed into a beautiful young woman, and he could more than imagine the thoughts that would run through any young man's mind. Thoughts that made Nolan want to protect his daughter even more.

He'd tried to explain how he felt to Heather before they'd driven home from the funeral, but he'd only made a bad situation worse. If the atmosphere in the car on the way to the church had been chilly, the drive home had plummeted to subzero.

The frost seemed to have settled on Kate, as well. She had averted her eyes whenever Nolan looked at her and gave curt one-word replies when she did happen to speak.

No doubt, she'd witnessed the blowup with Jimmy and watched as Heather had run from the hall. In fact, the entire congregation had been aware of the father-daughter tiff and was probably taking sides as to whether his parenting or Heather's willfulness was the problem.

He clenched his jaw, frustration growing within him. He'd "lost his cool," as Heather would say. Not something a grown man should do. Worse than that, he'd publicly disparaged his daughter.

Heather had always been a good child. Obedient, with a strong sense of right and wrong and an equally strong relationship with the Lord. But Olivia's death and the move had thrown her world into turmoil.

The sooner they could leave Mercy, the better. Yet before he left, he needed to expose the transplant tourist racket and shut it down for good.

Was he trying to do it all, without asking

the Lord's help?

Nolan bowed his head. *Dear Father God, You know the needs of my heart. Walk with me. Direct my steps. Let me see the things that matter and ignore any pettiness that may slow my way. Be my guide and my protection. In this I pray.*

Before he could say *Amen,* the phone rang. Nolan reached for the receiver. "Price."

"A cold wind's blowing in from the south." Dave Reynolds's voice filled the line.

"What'd you find?"

"Seems that little scientist you wanted me to check on stirred up a problem or two for Bannister Scientific."

Nolan sat up in his chair and jammed the phone closer to his ear. "What do you mean?"

"Bannister planned to merge with Southern Technology to become the largest research lab in the southeast. Your visitor questioned the way Southern Technology collected their data."

"So the merger's on hold?"

"Looks that way. If I were you, I'd keep an eye on Ms. Murphy. Too much of a coincidence to have a scientist land on your doorstep out of the clear blue. Especially when she's involved with transplant research."

"She's researching diabetes, Dave."

"Okay, boss. Whatever. But you were right about her growing up in El Paso. Salutatorian of her high school class. Undergrad scholarship to University of Texas at El Paso where she went on to get her master's. She's taken all the classes for her Ph.D. but never sat for her dissertation."

"That's strange. Did you find a reason?"

"She got her name tied in with a small-time drug ring. Some guy stole chemicals from her university research facility. Seems he was coming on to her in order to gain access to her lab and the chemicals she worked with."

"What happened?"

"The guy blew himself up. Your houseguest escaped. Said the guy attacked her. She ran, knocked over a candle and *boom!*"

"She wasn't charged?"

"Roger that." Dave paused when a beep sounded over the line. "I've got an incoming call from the nurse I told you about. We're supposed to see each other later this evening."

"Call me back on my cell."

Nolan hung up the phone and shook his head. Kate Murphy involved with a drug operation? She had told Nolan that God didn't listen to women who made a mess of their lives.

He had to convince her otherwise.

Kate heard Nolan stomp down to the basement. The man confused her. One minute, he was all heart when it came to his daughter. The next, he behaved like a vulture ready to attack. Whatever he'd said to Heather in the church hall had driven the girl back into her shell.

Probably had to do with Heather's friend. Kate had seen the way the girl had looked at Jimmy Ramos. Something was definitely in the air with those two.

She didn't blame Nolan for worrying. Hormones and a skewed sense of right and wrong got kids in trouble on a regular basis. Not that she thought Heather would do anything foolish, but even nice kids made bad decisions.

Nolan wanted what was best for his daughter. Unfortunately, he had tackled the situation today from the wrong direction. If he treated Heather as a budding adult, he might see more success than with the authoritative approach he had used at the church.

"Catch more flies with honey than vinegar," her grandfather used to say. Grandda. Now there was a man with a heart. And common sense, to boot.

What would he have said about *her* current predicament? Probably something like, "Katie-girl, you're getting deeper into something you know nothing about. Hightail it back to Atlanta first chance you get."

The fact that Nolan had asked Tracy to work for him a month ago bothered Kate. If Tina's condition had been growing progressively worse, she may have put in her notice. Yet neither Heather nor Nolan had said anything to indicate Tina was moving on.

Something about latex allergies picked at the back of Kate's mind. What was it? Blame it on her recent accident, but for the life of her she couldn't remember.

A few minutes searching an online medical site would provide the answers she needed. Surely, someone in this house owned a computer.

Kate found Heather in the kitchen, her nose in the fridge. "See anything good to eat?"

The girl whipped around, surprise written on her face.

"Hope I didn't scare you." Kate hurried to reassure her.

"I thought you were Dad."

"He went downstairs a few minutes ago."

"Figures." Heather turned her attention

back to the refrigerator. "How 'bout a ham sandwich?"

Kate wasn't hungry, but she did want to talk to Heather. "Sounds good. Where's the bread?"

"First drawer on your right." Heather placed the lunch meat and mustard on the counter while Kate grabbed the bread and poured two glasses of milk.

"I didn't think I was hungry," Kate admitted when her plate was empty.

Heather stuffed the last bite of sandwich into her mouth and nodded in agreement.

"So it's back to school tomorrow?" Kate asked.

"Yeah, but that's okay. The weekend's been *too* long."

And too painful, no doubt. "Who was that cute boy I saw you with today?" Kate hoped she didn't sound like she was prying.

The girl blushed ever so slightly. "Jimmy Ramos. He's a junior."

"Looks like you're pretty good friends."

Heather flipped her hair over her shoulder. "Dad says he's too old for me."

She'd heard that before. Eddie had been three years her senior — a source of contention between Kate and her grandfather. "Dads always worry about their daughters, don't they?"

Heather tilted her head. "Did your dad ever give you a hard time?"

"Yeah, but in a different way. My dad was . . . well, he had other things on his mind. But my grandfather —" Kate smiled at the memory. "He thought he knew exactly what I needed and wanted." She worked her finger around the rim of her glass. "Funny thing though. He was usually right."

Heather picked at the crumbs on her plate. "My dad means well. It's just . . ." She shrugged. "Sometimes I think he's afraid he'll lose me like we lost Mom."

"You mean that you'll get sick?"

The girl looked up. "Or that something worse might happen. When you see someone die — someone you love — it gets you all nervous and stuff. It's like you realize how easily life can end."

Suddenly, Kate understood the real issue. "I bet you worry about your dad."

"Sometimes, I get scared." The girl looked at Kate with serious eyes. "Like something will happen to him and I'll be all alone."

"Have you told him how you feel?"

Heather shook her head. "He doesn't listen to anything I say. He thinks Jimmy and I are getting way too serious. Jimmy stopped by the other night to see me. He heard Tina had died and wanted to make sure I was okay. Jimmy knows I'm not allowed to have friends over when Dad's not home. So he parked his car on one of the back trails."

Kate waited.

"Dad was at the funeral home, and when he came back and saw Jimmy standing on the porch, he raced after him and chased him through the woods."

"Jimmy ran away?" Kate asked.

"Yeah. But still." Heather fidgeted with her napkin. "Dad could have talked to *me* about it first."

Friday night. Had Jimmy Ramos brought Nolan to the creek the night of her crash?

"Your dad loves you very much, Heather."

"That's what he said at the funeral after he told Jimmy not to come over when I'm here alone."

Heather twisted a lock of her hair. "Jimmy makes good grades, and he tutors kids with math. He's a great guy."

"I'm sure he is, Heather. But dads don't like to see their daughters grow up. You know what would help?"

Heather shook her head.

"If you'd try to talk to your dad. I bet a lot of the problems would sort themselves out."

"I'm not sure. Let me pray about it."

Pray about it? Not the answer Kate expected. The young woman must have more faith than Kate realized.

Heather cleared the dishes from the table. "I'd better get back to my homework. Anything else you need?"

"Actually, I'd like to look something up on the Internet. Do you have a computer I could use?"

The girl pointed to a small alcove around the corner from the door. "Dad's got one hooked up back there. The password's taped on the counter under my mom's picture."

Once Heather left the kitchen, Kate scooted around the corner and dropped into the desk chair. She turned the computer on, hit the Internet icon and found the password just as Heather had said.

Nolan's wife stared back at Kate from the photo. Dressed in a sequined evening gown and long, sparkly earrings, Olivia looked elegant and poised as she stood in the midst of a large crowd of people.

Kate tugged at the baggy sweats she wore and, on a whim, typed in Olivia's name.

Page after page of sites scrolled across the monitor. Seemed Ms. Price was a celebrity in her own right.

Kate clicked on a news article dated eight months ago.

"Olivia Price . . . died Thursday. Price's work in cinema production has been heralded as realistic portrayals of . . ."

Kate's eyes darted over the text.

"Survived by husband Nolan and daughter Heather . . . funeral to be held . . . in lieu of flowers the family requested donations be made to World Watch."

Kate had heard of World Watch. A Christian-based organization that dealt with global health issues. Recently, their focus had been the illegal sale of human organs.

Nolan said his wife had died from an infection following surgery. Could she have been an organ recipient? If so, why hadn't he mentioned —

"You could have asked," a voice said behind her.

Startled, Kate turned to find Nolan staring down at her, his eyes as black as coal.

"I would have told you anything you wanted to know about Olivia."

Heat swept over Kate, a burning sensation that had to do with embarrassment and shame and a little frustration at being found out. "I . . . I . . ."

How had she gotten herself into this pickle? "I'm sorry. It's just that your daughter's pain touched me deeply today. I thought if I knew a little about your wife, I might be able to reach out to Heather."

"Reach out?"

Kate cleared her throat. "As I told you yesterday, Nolan, Heather's a beautiful girl, but she has a lot on her shoulders."

"And you're ready to help her carry her load?"

Was the man faulting her interest in his child? "I'd like to be her friend."

"For what, two or three more days? Before you leave Mercy and head back to Atlanta?"

Why was he so upset? "You're right, of course. I was planning on Tuesday, but I could leave tomorrow, if you want."

He let out an exasperated lungful of air. "That's not what I meant. It's just that Heather's had so many people cut out of her life. She doesn't need another fly-by-night friend. What she needs is stability."

Then why'd you leave California? Kate wanted to ask. But she bit her tongue, knowing Nolan was right. She couldn't offer Heather more than a day or two of her time. She needed to head back to Atlanta and her work. Not that she was a hundred percent certain she still had a job.

"I can't make any promises to you or your daughter, Nolan. But I still want to be Heather's friend."

Scooting the chair back, Kate stood and

found herself standing inches from Nolan, a little too close for comfort.

He hastily took a step back as she edged sideways, accidentally putting weight on her injured leg. She winced as a sharp jab sliced through her knee.

"Olivia must have been a very special woman," Kate said, once the pain subsided. "I can only imagine the devastation you and Heather had to face with her death and then with Tina's."

Nolan made no comment. He just stood there, staring down at her, hands on his hips, jaw clenched, brow raised and not a sound issuing from his lips.

The silence made her pulse race even faster. *Fill the void, Kate. Say something. Anything.*

Without forethought, she opened her mouth and the words spilled out. "I hope my being here hasn't affected the rather tenuous relationship you and Heather currently seem to be having. In my opinion, a little more talking and a little less lecturing might be what the two of you need."

A muscle in Nolan's neck twitched. "You always kick a guy when he's down?"

For an instant, Kate thought he was going to smile, but his mouth took a downward turn.

Once again, she had messed up big-time.

"Like you said yesterday, Nolan, my timing's off." She reached for the crutches. "It's late. I need to shut up and go to bed."

Shoving the crutches under her arms, Kate hobbled back to her room and closed the door hard behind her. She'd had enough of Nolan Price for one day. The man was wound too tightly. He loved his daughter, but he had a problem communicating with her, and he seemed to object to Kate's attempt to help.

She shook her head and let out a deep sigh. He'd probably claim she was shoving her weight around where it didn't belong.

Maybe she was. Underline the *didn't belong* part.

Time to pack up and go home. Tomorrow, she'd make some calls and try to snag a ride back to Atlanta.

Then she remembered her cross.

Nolan stood at the computer until Kate left the kitchen and the door to her bedroom slammed shut. He was overreacting to everything these days. But when he saw Kate looking at Olivia's obituary, something had snapped inside. Who *was* this woman who had dropped into their lives?

As Nolan closed out of the Web, his cell

rang. "Price."

"Nolan, it's Dave. I just got off the phone with the little LPN. Seems they're preparing Dr. Hira's after-hours patient for a liver transplant. Guess where the surgery will be performed?"

"India. Which means a layover in Mercy. Did you get a name, Dave?"

"The patient's real name is Barb Preston. Fifty-two years old. Married to the head of Preston Studios."

"Michael Preston? He's supposedly involved with a young starlet."

"Roger that. Probably why Mrs. Preston took a bottle of acetaminophen."

"Who found her?"

"The maid called 911. Mrs. Preston survived but her liver didn't. Guess she's decided to give life a second chance. She's booked on a flight to Atlanta tomorrow morning."

"I'll drive to the airport after Heather leaves for school. Any idea the name Mrs. Preston will be using in Georgia?"

"Sally Armstrong."

"Good. That'll make it easier. I'll be on the lookout for a limo driver holding a sign for Ms. Armstrong."

"Too bad you can't meet the plane at the gate."

"No such luck since 9/11. Olivia said the limo driver met her near baggage claim. If everything goes as planned, I'll be able to spot our tourist when she hooks up with the driver. Mrs. Preston might provide information we could use against the center. Bottom line though, I'll try to convince her to turn around and go home."

"Let me know what happens," Dave said. "Anything else we need to talk about tonight?"

"Only that Tina left me a voice mail. She found something in the woods."

"A tie-in with the doc's presurgery treatment?"

"Could be. All I know is she died a few hours later."

"Be careful, Nolan."

"We're close, Dave."

"Yeah, but nothing's worth your life."

NINE

Kate couldn't sleep. She tossed and turned, causing her leg to scream in protest. Lie still, her mind commanded, but her heart stewed in turmoil, and slumber eluded her until well after the first light of dawn peered through her window.

A tap-tap-tap at her door pulled her from the first true sleep she'd managed to capture all night.

"Who is it?" she called, raising her head from the pillow and glancing at the clock. Seven-fifteen.

"It's Nolan. Heather just left for school, and I've been called out of town on business."

Kate swung her bare feet over the side of the bed, reached for the terry bathrobe and shuffled to the door, hoping her disarray and morning breath wouldn't knock Nolan over.

She pulled the door open and found him

leaning against the jamb. A surprised look washed over his face as she appeared in place of the door.

"Sorry to wake you." He smiled and she couldn't help returning the grin.

Tugging a hand through her tussled hair, she realized too late she should have kept the door closed.

"I wasn't asleep." She stretched the truth. She *had* been awake most of the night. She wouldn't mention that she'd just drifted off seemingly minutes before he'd knocked.

She avoided his gaze by looking down and studying her toes, wiggling them against the floor as if they suddenly demanded her undivided attention.

She didn't know if she should chance another glance upward the way her heart thumped against her rib cage. She'd been caught off guard. The accident and lack of sleep went into the mix, causing her pulse to race. Medically, she understood her body's response. But as she looked up at Nolan, she knew medicine had nothing to do with the way she felt. She was falling for him despite herself.

Nolan cleared his throat and pulled his hand from the door frame. "Something unexpected came up, and I have to be out of town until early evening. You're staying another day, aren't you?"

Did he want her to leave? "If you don't mind."

He held up a hand, palm out. "Not a problem. In fact, I'd appreciate it if you *could* stay. That way Heather won't be alone. She gets home from school at three-fifteen."

Why hadn't he said that in the first place? "Of course. Don't worry. I'll be here."

Relief washed over his face. "I've got a fresh pot of coffee brewing in the kitchen. Food's in the fridge. Help yourself."

He nodded his thanks, then stepped away.

Kate closed the door and leaned against the thick oak. She prided herself on being in control, but standing close to Nolan had made her usually stable world swing topsy-turvy.

She'd give herself twenty-four more hours in Mercy. No longer. She needed to find her cross and get back to Atlanta where she acted like a normal adult and not some lovestruck preteen.

One more day. She shook her head. A lot could happen in that amount of time.

Nolan's breath hung in the cold morning air as he stepped out the back door and almost ran headlong into the sheriff's wife.

"Edith?"

"Morning, Mr. Price." The woman held a plate of brownies in her outstretched hand. "Ms. Agnes wanted me to bring these over first thing. She thought your houseguest might enjoy something sweet."

Nolan took the plate. "Ms. Agnes having trouble sleeping?"

The nurse nodded. "Baking calms her nerves. Sue Ann had a rough night, as well."

"Tell Agnes thanks."

As she started to walk away, Nolan noticed the empty drive and called after her, "Edith, where'd you park your car?"

She turned to stare at him for a long minute. "On the main road. I didn't want to block you in." She blinked. "I wasn't snooping around."

"Of course you weren't."

Strange comment. Made him think she had been doing exactly that.

Nolan shook off the thought.

Reentering the kitchen, he placed the brownies on the table, then headed to the garage where his SUV sat parked next to Tina's two-door sedan. The sheriff had brought Tina's car back late Friday afternoon, a few hours before Kate had crashed into the creek and into Nolan's life.

He glanced at the spare tire on the left rear wheel. Doc Samuels claimed Tina had died due to an allergic reaction while changing her tire.

Could he trust the doc's diagnosis? Nolan needed to find out the truth.

His cell phone rang as he turned onto the main highway, heading toward Atlanta. "Price."

"Sir, it's Hank Evans."

The mechanic at Mercy Automotive. "Thanks for calling me back, Hank."

"Pauline just left to clean Wade Green's home. She'll get those pictures for you."

Nolan shoved the cell closer to his ear. "Did you tell her to be careful?"

"Yes, sir. Pauline wants to get to the bottom of it, just like you do. She knew I was upset after what I'd seen. Like I told you before, Ray's got the only tow service in the area. He brings the cars back to the garage."

"The vehicles involved in accidents?"

"Yes, sir. That's right. Only I started thinking we were having too many wrecks. That's why I decided to do a little snooping."

"And you discovered someone had tampered with the tie rods?"

"Tampered with a lot of things. I checked the last five cars that wrecked on the mountain roads. Nothing accidental about any of those crashes."

Nolan pulled in a deep breath. "Did you

tell Ray?"

"No, sir. Kept it to myself. Didn't want the boss to think I was a troublemaker, jobs being hard to come by like they are in this area. Once Pauline told me what she saw on the funeral director's computer, well, I knew bad things were happening in Mercy. Lucky for me, you stopped by the garage that day."

Lucky for Nolan, as well. A few subtle questions and Hank had poured out his fears. "You never told me how Pauline accessed the computer file."

"Accident, pure and simple. Mrs. Green had a doctor's appointment and was gone that day. Mr. Green was working from home. He stepped into the kitchen to get a cup of coffee. Pauline wanted to tidy up while he was in the other room. Guess his computer had gone to screen saver. When she was dusting, she must have touched the keyboard. The photo appeared on the monitor."

"And Pauline recognized the body?"

"Yes, sir. That was the hard part. Pauline knew Marty Jackson. He was kin on her mama's side. The guy had a wild streak and didn't amount to much. Still, like Pauline says, he was family."

"I'm sorry, Hank."

141

"Funny thing. Marty's folks had visited him in the hospital, and he seemed to be doing okay. Next they knew, he had a heart attack."

"Did he have a history of heart disease?"

"Marty was strong as an ox. The day of the accident, he'd been hunting on the far side of Mercy Mountain. Told his dad he'd seen something suspicious before the brakes gave out on his pickup."

Had Marty been silenced because of what he'd seen in the woods? Just like Tina? "Did Doc Samuels pay for Marty's cremation?"

"That's right. Mountain people don't cotton to cremation. They like to bury their dead, but the Jacksons are poor folks. They had to take what the doc offered."

Lloyd Samuels knew how to cover his trail. A body burned to ash left no evidence.

"Were there any witnesses to the crash?"

"No, sir. Nobody saw nothin'."

Nolan sighed, his heart heavy. There was a pattern to the so-called accidents. Severed tie rods. Isolated mountain roads. No witnesses. "I can't let Pauline get caught in the middle."

"Don't worry, Mr. Price. Pauline worked in an office before we met. She's real smart with computers. She'll be careful."

Much as Nolan needed the photos, he

didn't want another woman put in danger. "I don't like it, Hank. Tell her it's a no-go. Eventually, I'll uncover enough evidence to notify the authorities. They'll get a court order to access Wade's computer."

"I'll tell her, but doubt Pauline'll listen. Besides, those pictures might be gone by then. I should have more information for you once I check out that Mustang we pulled from the creek."

Doubtful anyone involved with the accidents would have tampered with Kate's car, but better safe than sorry.

"And if you don't mind, Mr. Price, I'll stop by your house a little later and drop off the clothing we found in the trunk of your houseguest's car."

"I'm sure Ms. Murphy will appreciate getting her things back. Thanks for your help, Hank. And thank Pauline for me."

Nolan snapped the cell shut. If what Hank said proved true, at least one physician tied to the Beverly Hills Center may be dealing not only in a transplant tourist scheme, but in murder, as well.

When Kate heard Nolan's car leave the driveway, she dressed quickly and headed to the kitchen. A plate of brownies sat on the table. She grabbed one, poured a cup of coffee and scooted into the alcove where she booted up the computer.

Nolan had said he'd be gone until evening. Ample time to search the Web. She needed information on latex allergies to understand how Tina had died.

Throughout the morning, Kate reviewed online medical sources. Dr. Samuels was right. Latex had become a growing problem throughout the general population, as well as with the medical community. At noon, she fixed a ham-and-cheese sandwich, reached for another brownie and continued her search.

A list of foods that produced cross-reactions in latex-sensitive individuals flashed on the screen. Bananas. Kiwi. Chestnuts. Avocados.

Avocados?

Guacamole had always been a part of Tina's daily diet.

Before Kate could read further, a vehicle pulled into the driveway. The doorbell rang, and a nervous twitter scurried down Kate's spine. Nolan's house was far from town and sat back from the road.

She shook her head and reached for her crutch. *None of that nonsense.*

Maybe the caller was the pregnant woman who seemed to be the recipient of Nolan's generosity, given out of the goodness of his heart, no doubt. Could there be another reason?

No use second-guessing something that wasn't her business.

Another rap sounded just before Kate inched the door open and peered outside where a tall, beefy man about Kate's age shivered in his shirtsleeves. *Hank* was embroidered over his left breast pocket, *Mercy Automotive* on the right.

"Afternoon, ma'am." He bent to pick up a plastic bag resting at his feet. "I'm Hank Evans, from the auto shop. We're working on your car. Ray wanted me to bring these things by."

He held out the bag. "They're the clothes from your car. My wife washed them. Said you'd had enough problems, didn't need to face creek muck on your things with Miss Tina passing and all."

He bowed his head as if in deference to the dead, before continuing. "Pauline said to tell you the overnight bag didn't make it. Guess it was waterlogged. But the clothes are okay."

His sincerity touched Kate. "Thank you, Hank, and please thank your wife for me. That was so nice of her."

Hank's face broke into a wide grin.

"Shoot, ma'am. Pauline always tries to be neighborly." He placed the bag inside the door.

"I'd like to pay for her time and effort," Kate said.

"No, ma'am. Pauline wouldn't take no money. She just wanted to help."

Kate waved goodbye as the man double-timed down the drive to where his pickup was parked. Closing the door, she carried the bag to her room and unpacked the stack of clothing Pauline had washed and ironed.

Items from Kate's previous life, before Tina's call, before the crash, before her heart went jittery whenever Nolan strayed too close.

Kate changed into gray slacks and a blue sweater, and fastened the immobilizer over her pant leg, feeling a bit more human in her own clothing.

As she left her room, she thought of a way to thank Hank and his wife. Locating a telephone directory in the kitchen, Kate looked up the Evans's address and the number for a local florist, then ordered a large bouquet delivered to their home as a token of her appreciation.

When she hung up, another thought came to mind. Kate found the number for Mercy MedClinic and dialed.

"Laboratory, please," she said to the receptionist who answered.

"I'll connect you. One moment, please." The operator forwarded her call.

"Lab, Stacy."

Kate hesitated. As fast as news traveled in Mercy, she didn't want anyone questioning why a newcomer would be making inquiries. Just so the lab tech wouldn't notice the omission of Kate's name, she said, "Stacy, I'm calling from Bannister Scientific. We're doing a study on laboratory compliance with OSHA standards on universal precautions."

"Ah, I'm only the phlebotomist. Maybe I should get my supervisor."

"That won't be necessary. This will only take a minute. What would you estimate is the percentage of time your laboratory personnel wear gloves when drawing patient blood?"

"We always wear gloves, ma'am."

"And those would be latex?" Kate asked.

"That's correct."

"Do you stock any other type of gloves, such as those made of nitrile?"

"Nitrile?"

"For lab workers allergic to latex," Kate explained.

Stacy hesitated. "No one has that problem,

that I'm aware of."

"One more question, Stacy. In the last six to eight months, have any of your patients been sensitive to latex?"

"No, ma'am. Not that I've heard. Like I said, we've got one type glove and one type only. That's latex."

Kate hung up with a sick feeling in the pit of her stomach. In order to verify Tina had had an allergy to latex, Dr. Samuels would have drawn her blood and tested her antibody production. Surely, he would have notified the lab of a latex-sensitive patient so they could have stocked at least one box of non-latex gloves.

Kate hobbled over to the refrigerator, tugged on the door and did a quick search of the crispers.

Two heads of lettuce, a pint of grape tomatoes, one cucumber and two onions. But no avocados.

Maybe Tina had given up her passion for guacamole.

Peering out the window, Kate noticed the detached garage. Nolan had said Tina had lived upstairs.

Crutch in hand, Kate grabbed the set of keys hanging on the peg by the door and headed outside.

The cold winter air cut though her

sweater. Silly not to have put on a coat, but a sense of urgency pushed her forward.

Kate found the side door to the garage unlocked and stepped inside. The smell of gasoline and exhaust hung in the air. A two-door Honda sat parked in the far stall.

Fire-engine red. Tina's favorite color.

Kate checked the tires. A small spare was on the left rear wheel.

About time Kate accepted the explanation everyone in town seemed to offer for Tina's death and stop this stupid attempt to play private eye.

"Let the dead rest in peace," she har-rumphed.

Stepping away from the car, she eyed the stairway to the second floor and thought of her grandfather's cross. Might as well check Tina's apartment. If her search proved successful, she could leave Mercy and put the last couple of days behind her.

Using the handrail and crutch for support, Kate climbed the stairs, one painful step at a time. Slow going, but when she arrived at the top landing, she fished into her pocket, pulled out the keys and tried the first three. The lock held firm.

She glanced over her shoulder at the steep ascent she'd just climbed. Getting down would be even more of a challenge.

One key left.

She stuck it into the keyhole. The lock turned.

Drawing in a deep breath, she pushed the door open.

TEN

Kate stepped into the garage apartment and looked around, taking in the double bed, oak dresser and writing table with desk chair. An overstuffed recliner sat in the corner. A small bronze cross hung on the wall above the desk.

Lowering herself to the bed, Kate ran her hand over the knobby spread and touched the satin pillow propped against the headboard. Seek and Ye Shall Find was stitched across the fabric.

A photo sat on the desk. A snapshot Kate had taken of Tina, her mom and Eddie. Their arms entwined, the family resemblance so profound Kate could hardly pull her eyes from the threesome staring back at her.

Seek and ye shall find. Would she find the cross?

Hobbling to the dresser, she pulled open the top drawer. Neatly folded clothing. A few bracelets. The pearl necklace Mrs. Espinosa had worn to church each Sunday.

But no cross.

A search of the other drawers proved equally disappointing. Kate glanced again at the photo of Tina. Raven-black hair, laughing eyes, a wide grin as if she didn't have a care in the world.

Kate remembered the Sunday afternoon when Tina had asked her to snap the photo. Life had been good then. Kate and Eddie had been dating for over a year. She'd given him her grandfather's cross. Eddie had asked enough pointed questions about diamonds and her preference in rings that she felt certain he was ready to pop the question.

He'd also asked not-so-pointed questions about the chemicals she used in her lab, chemicals that could be cooked into a drug so pervasive even she didn't recognize the signs in the man she'd thought she loved.

She'd been too caught up in the moment to recognize the signs of addiction.

Some people said God only gave what you could handle. Kate shook her head. What a lie. He'd given Kate too much heartache. Too much pain.

She shoved her chin up with determination. Not the time for memories. She needed to keep searching.

In the bottom desk drawer, she found a daily journal. Flipping through the pages, Kate recognized Tina's bold script and hesitated. Should she intrude on her former friend's privacy?

Kate thought back to the phone call, Tina's frightened voice and her death just hours later. Any information might help explain what had happened that fateful day.

Nolan is a good man, Tina wrote. *He's thoughtful and generous, and taking care of Heather and his house hardly seems like work.*

Another entry. *Thank you, Lord, for leading me to this family so that our paths could cross exactly at the time I most needed a helping hand. With Eddie gone and Mom in the nursing home . . .*

Nursing home? Had Mrs. Espinosa been ill?

A rumble sounded in the distance.

Kate slanted a glance at the clock on the desk. Three-ten. Nolan had said Heather would be home by three-fifteen.

As Kate lowered the journal to the drawer, her eyes locked on a slip of paper. A check Nolan had signed made out to Tina Espinosa. But the amount —

Kate let out the breath she had been holding. The check was for five thousand dollars.

Why such a large sum of money? Ms. Agnes had said Nolan gave money to Tracy Farrington.

How many women did he support? And for what reason? What did he get out of it?

Kate shoved off the thought. Everything pointed to Tina's conversion and a life focused on Christ. That probably explained Nolan's charitability.

Another rumble. Kate peered out the window. A yellow school bus crested the distant hill.

Kate shoved the journal into the waistband of her slacks, pulled the sweater over the bulge and slammed the desk drawer.

Nothing made sense. Gifts of money, Tina's death, a supposed allergy.

Kate would read the journal tonight in the privacy of her room. Perhaps she'd learn something that would untangle the web of confusion surrounding Tina's death.

Nolan pulled the foam cup to his lips and took a sip of coffee he'd purchased at a kiosk in the airport atrium, the burned dregs from the bottom of the pot, laced with enough caffeine to keep him wired for a week.

Surveillance wasn't his strong suit. He would express his thanks to Dave next time they talked for all the long days and nights he'd patiently waited for someone to appear.

Earlier in the day, Nolan had staked a claim on an area between the north and south terminal baggage claims. Since then, he'd watched a steady flow of passengers ride the escalators from the shuttle train off-load area to the main concourse.

A line of drivers stood nearby, holding cardboard placards, identifying passengers they were waiting to transport. Two and a half hours ago, a tall, slender man dressed in a black tux and bow tie had taken up his post, carrying a sign for S. Armstrong.

Undoubtedly, the limo driver who would drive Barb Preston, aka Sally Armstrong, to Mercy.

Taking another slug of his lukewarm coffee, Nolan glanced at his watch. Heather would be home from school soon. Kate would be there to greet her at the door.

He smiled, remembering how Kate had looked this morning when she'd opened the guest room door. He'd caught her by surprise from the expression on her face. The way his gut had tightened had surprised him, as well.

A widower with a teenage daughter shouldn't be smitten by a pretty face. He was acting like a schoolboy in love.

Love?

The thought threw him. He shook himself back to the present, almost missing the fashionably dressed middle-aged woman who stepped off the escalator and walked directly toward the limo driver.

Nolan's surveillance had finally paid off.

He edged forward, hoping to reach the woman before she and the driver left the area.

To Nolan's right, a child hopped across the tile floor. "Step on a crack, break your mother's back," the boy chanted.

Without warning, the child lunged sideways. His small arms flailed through the air, hitting the cup Nolan was holding and knocking it from his hand.

The coffee splashed over a passerby. "What the —" the man groused as the tepid liquid splattered his leg.

"I'm so sorry," Nolan said, frustrated by his own failure to prevent the spill.

The man held up his hand, palm out. "S'alright."

Nolan nodded and pressed on. "Ms. Armstrong?"

The woman ignored the name and scurried off into the crowd.

"You looking for her, too?" the limo driver asked when Nolan stopped short.

"Ah —" He'd probably said too much already.

The driver shook his head. "Shoot, that lady just wanted the time. The Ms. Armstrong I'm waiting for should have been on a flight from LAX two hours ago. Doesn't appear she's coming in today. My shift's over. Don't know about you, but I'm calling it a day."

Had Barb Preston, posing as Sally Armstrong, missed her flight? Or perhaps she'd had second thoughts about undergoing a liver transplant in a foreign country. The reality was backing out might have saved her life. But Nolan needed information the woman would be able to provide.

He let out a lungful of pent-up breath as the driver walked away.

Win some. Lose some.

In Nolan's opinion, today was definitely a loss.

A sharp pain in Kate's left leg signaled she had descended the garage stairs too quickly. Wincing, she hobbled into the kitchen at the same moment the front door flew open. Kate leaned on her crutch and scooted into the hallway, nearly colliding with Heather as she bounded through the foyer.

"I've got a real problem, and you just *have* to let me go back to school." The words spilled from Heather's mouth.

"Ms. Watson said the algebra problems at the end of the chapter weren't due this week. At least that's what I *thought* she said. Then on the bus, Becca said they were due *tomorrow*. Ms. Watson's counting them double, and I'm borderline between an A and a B, so if I don't have the work done, then —"

She tugged her right hand through her blond hair and pulled more air into her lungs. "It'd be like the end of the world if I got a B just 'cause I didn't bring my book home, and Becca said she could get her mom's car and drive me back to school —"

Kate held up her hand. "You're talking too fast, Heather."

The girl's brow furrowed.

"You left a book at school?" Kate tried to get a handle on the problem.

Nolan's daughter jerked her head up and down. "And I *have* to do those problems by tomorrow or I'll get an F. Becca said she could drive me."

A hastily devised taxi service didn't sound like a good idea to Kate. "I doubt your dad would approve."

Heather let out a sigh of exasperation. "He wouldn't want me to flunk."

"You can explain it to your teacher tomorrow. I'm sure she'll understand."

The girl's eyes widened. "No way. Ms. Watson's an ogre. She never accepts excuses. You've gotta believe me."

At least Heather was conscientious about her schoolwork. "Maybe your dad can swing by school on his way into town," Kate suggested.

Heather's shoulders drooped ever so slightly. "He'd tell me to deal with it and face the consequences of my forgetfulness."

Kate almost laughed. Although she doubted Nolan would be quite that blunt, she could see him using logical consequences to teach the teen a lesson.

"We could take Tina's car." Heather looked down at Kate's injured leg. "I've got my learner's, and Tina always let me drive whenever we went into town. We'd be back in no time. Please?"

Kate understood Heather's sense of urgency. Teenagers viewed everything as immediate and personal. In Heather's mind, not having her math book to do her homework was an astronomical problem. And one that had to be solved without delay.

"I'm a good driver. Cross my heart," Heather added to seal the deal.

"We'll call your dad and ask him."

"But he said he wouldn't be home until late. Why don't we just surprise him? He always says I need more practice, although recently he's never had time. I know it'll be okay."

Kate held up her hand. "We'll talk to your father first."

"All right," Heather finally agreed. "I'll call him while you get a coat."

As Heather dialed her dad's cell, Kate limped into the guest room. Removing the journal from her waistband, she dropped the book into the nightstand drawer and tucked her credit card, driver's license and some small change into her pocket. After slipping on the jacket Heather had loaned her, Kate returned to the kitchen, crutch in hand, just as the teen hung up the phone and reached for a brownie.

"I left a message on Dad's voice mail. But I know he'd say it was okay." She smiled with confidence and took a bite of the rich chocolate.

Heather had told Kate her problem in hopes she could be of help. The last thing Kate wanted was to close the door of communication that had just opened.

"Grab your learner's permit and the keys to the car."

"I've got them." Heather reached for the doorknob, then stopped and gave Kate a lopsided grin. "Guess someone brought your clothes back."

"Hank from the garage."

"You look nice."

A compliment, and perhaps a sign the door might push open even further. Heather's guard had dropped. Learning to drive was an important step in growing up. Surely Nolan wouldn't mind if they made a quick trip to Heather's school.

Plus, Kate might learn a little more about the reclusive widower. The guy was hard to read. Not that she was interested.

Nolan left the terminal and headed back to his car, hoping to get through the city before the worst of the afternoon traffic.

An accident and road construction turned the drive into a nightmare.

An hour later and still snarled in traffic, he pulled off the highway to refuel. As he climbed back into his SUV, he reached for his cell. *One missed call.*

Nolan clicked the view button. *Home.* Pushing speed dial, he waited for Heather or Kate to pick up on the other end.

No answer.

He disconnected and dialed Dave.

"Remind me never to drive anywhere in Atlanta after 3:00 p.m."

"Traffic couldn't be as bad as L.A."

"Doesn't matter which side of the country you're on, gridlock is gridlock."

"I was getting ready to call you. The LPN left me a voice mail. Seems Mrs. Preston missed her plane."

"Any idea why?"

"Your guess is as good as mine."

Nolan filled Dave in on his uneventful day at the airport.

The P.I. chuckled. "Sounds like you clocked in a few hours of surveillance."

"I'm becoming a pro, although it's not my favorite way to pass the day."

"I hear you," Dave agreed.

"Call me later, if you learn anything new." Nolan disconnected, then hit the home listing. The answering machine kicked in on the sixth ring.

An anxious tingle crept up his neck.

Where were Heather and Kate?

Turning the key in the ignition, Nolan stepped on the accelerator. He needed to get back to Mercy ASAP.

ELEVEN

Kate waited in the car while Heather entered the high school and exited a few minutes later, math book in hand.

"Thanks so much," Heather gushed as she climbed into the driver's seat and tossed the text into the back.

Kate smiled. "Glad everything worked out."

The teen buckled the seat belt over her chest. Once the traffic cleared, she pulled onto the county road, accelerated to the speed limit and kept the car at an even forty miles per hour.

"You're a good driver," Kate encouraged. "And you stay within the speed limit."

Heather's cheeks flushed with the praise. "Dad says I still have a lot to learn. But I got an A in my driving safety class at school."

"Your dad knows time behind the wheel is important."

Heather nodded and threw a quick smile in Kate's direction. "Let's go home through town. You haven't seen anything in Mercy, except the clinic and church."

"Great! You can give me the grand tour." Kate smiled, enjoying the new relaxed air in the car.

Heather was like all kids. They longed for attention and affirmation and someone to listen to their problems. Heather had more than her fair share. Leaving L.A. must have been hard.

"I bet you miss your friends from California."

"Yeah, maybe a couple." Heather chewed on her lip. "But the kids here welcomed me right away. I never felt like I belonged back in L.A."

"In what way?"

Heather shrugged. "I don't know. Maybe 'cause they were kind of fast."

"Involved in things you weren't interested in?" Kate offered.

"A lot of kids did drugs. Sex was pretty common. Plus, they had lots of money, and their parents let them stay out late."

Now wasn't Heather sounding very adult. "Different from Mercy?"

Heather nodded. "Around here, morality means something. Sure, some of the kids get carried away, but most of them are working hard to get good grades so they can get scholarships to college."

"Then moving to Mercy was a good thing?"

"I guess. Except Dad's been more protective than he ever was in California."

"Any idea why?"

"Probably 'cause it's hard to let go."

Once again, the girl's maturity impressed Kate. She knew adults who weren't as savvy.

"I promised you a tour of Mercy." Heather pointed to a small white clapboard house that sat back from the road. "That's where Tracy Farrington lives with her sister, Pauline, and Pauline's husband, Hank, who brought your stuff back today."

So Tracy's sister was the woman who'd washed Kate's clothes? "I talked to Tracy at the funeral. She and your dad must be good friends."

Heather shrugged. "Sort of, I guess. Dad met her at Bible Study."

Heather didn't mention that Tracy would soon fill Tina's position as housekeeper.

"The next place is Mr. Hawkins's farm," the girl continued.

"Wasn't that where they found Tina?"

Heather pointed to a narrow trail that curved through the tall trees. "Yeah, down that dirt road."

"Where's the path lead?"

Heather's hands tightened on the wheel. "No place."

She didn't sound all that convincing. "Someone live out there?" Kate pushed.

"There's an old abandoned cabin, that's all."

Heather raised her right hand, tugged at a lock of hair and flipped the strand behind her ear. "Ms. Agnes Heartwell lives in the big house on top of Mercy Mountain." Heather pointed to the large ranch situated on the hillside, overlooking the valley below. "She lives there with her handicapped daughter."

"Agnes mentioned Sue Ann's accident when I talked to her at the funeral."

Heather pursed her lips, looking older than her fifteen years. "Sad, but Ms. Agnes talks like Sue Ann will get better. That's what families always think. Only sometimes there's just no hope."

Kate's heart went out to Heather. She had been through so much. Losing a mom was always hard. Kate had been a baby when her own mother had died.

First steps, first grade, first date . . . all with only her grandfather at her side. A good man with a big heart, but for all the love he had showered upon Kate, she still grieved for her mother.

"My mom died when I was a baby," Kate said, surprised by the emotion she heard in her own voice.

Heather glanced at her. "You never knew your mother?"

"My grandfather raised me."

"What about your dad?"

Hard to talk about the reality of their relationship. "My dad didn't want to be a parent. I'm not sure he realized what being a dad was all about." The truth hurt.

Kate glanced at the countryside rolling past the window. "When I was little I used to think if I was really good, he'd come back."

Heather nodded. "Like maybe it was your fault he went away?"

"Exactly. Still kind of bothers me."

Heather kept her eyes on the road ahead. "When my mom died, I thought I'd done something wrong. Then I blamed my dad. He had to leave on business. I begged him not to go. He wasn't away long, only it was too long for Mom."

Kate rubbed the girl's shoulder. "I'm sorry, honey."

Heather wiped her hand across her cheek and sniffed before she spoke again. "Mom had been in India, working on a film about poor people. She got sick and had to have surgery, only she didn't tell us until she came home."

India? One of the countries where World Watch was trying to stop the illegal sale of organs.

"Your mom had to have an operation while she was in India?" Kate pressed, hoping to learn a little more about Olivia.

Heather nodded. "Dad must have told you about her transplant."

"He mentioned surgery."

"I know Dad tries to do what's right, but when my mother needed him . . . when I needed him . . ." Heather swallowed hard.

Kate remained silent.

"Ever since Mom died, he's had a tough time understanding me." Heather glanced at Kate. "Guess we have that in common."

Kate nodded. A small wall had crumbled between them. Heather had shared her heart and the pain she carried. Kate was grateful for her openness.

A comfortable silence settled over the car for the next few miles. At the second four-way stop, Heather signaled, turned left and, half a mile later, drove into downtown Mercy.

"The Corner Coffee Shop is at the end of

the block," she said. "Let's stop for a latte."

"Sounds great." Kate pointed to the drugstore two doors from the corner. "I need to pick up some makeup and toilet articles. I'll meet you in a few minutes."

In spite of a hurt leg and crutch, Kate quickly found the items she needed, charged them to her credit card and hobbled to the coffee shop. Opening the door, she inhaled the rich aroma of freshly ground coffee beans and spied Heather, carrying two steaming mugs to a round table.

"My treat." Kate grabbed the check and handed it along with a few bills to the clerk behind the counter. The shop bustled with customers, many sipping coffee topped with whipped cream and sprinkles of mocha. Kate recognized a few of the folks from the funeral who nodded to her as she settled into a chair.

Kate took the first sip of her latte, enjoying the rich, creamy froth, and looked up as the outside door opened.

A man — late twenties, square face with broad shoulders and a buzz haircut — stepped into the shop. He wore a navy-blue jacket, and when he turned, the letters *MFD* were visible on the back.

Mercy Fire Department.

Jimmy Ramos followed the fireman inside.

Heather noticed the boy immediately and slid from her chair. "I want to say hello to a friend of mine."

Kate could sense the girl's excitement. Nothing like young love with its breathless rush of adrenaline.

Exactly how she'd felt in the beginning with Eddie. But somewhere along the way, that enthusiasm had been replaced, first with excuses and then betrayal.

Kate took another sip of latte and pushed away the memories.

Some things should remain buried.

Heather and the boy chattered as if they hadn't seen each other in days. The fireman stood next to them in line, occasionally laughing at their conversation. He ordered two coffees and rumpled Jimmy's hair when the younger boy tried to pay.

To-go mugs in hand, they walked Heather back to the table.

"Kate, this is Jimmy Ramos and his bother Miguel," Heather said.

Kate shook Miguel's hand and smiled up at Jimmy. "Didn't I see you at the funeral yesterday?" she asked, noticing Jimmy's dimples and large brown eyes.

The boy blushed as he glanced quickly at the floor and then back at her. "Yes, ma'am. Wanted to pay my respects. Miss Tina was a nice lady."

"Heather told us that you knew Tina," Miguel said.

Kate nodded. "A long time ago."

"Shame what happened. Couldn't believe it when we got the call."

Kate wrinkled her brow. "What call?"

"Friday," Miguel continued. "Fire Department answered the emergency."

"You were on duty?" Kate asked.

"That's right. Wish we could have made a difference." He shook his head sadly.

"Dr. Samuels said Tina had an anaphylactic reaction. Evidently, she was allergic to latex."

"That's what they told us after the doc looked her over."

"I suppose you guys carry latex-free gloves?"

Miguel nodded. "Sure. No point using them, though. Tina died before we got there. Nothing left to do but transport her body back to Mercy."

The finality of Miguel's words cut into Kate's heart.

Tina had died on a lonely stretch of back road. But had her death been caused by an allergic reaction?

After the two brothers said goodbye, a strange sense of uneasiness swept over Kate.

She turned to survey the coffee shop. Most of the customers chatted amicably at their tables.

In the corner, one woman sat alone. Fidgeting with the napkin in her lap, she raised her eyes and met Kate's gaze.

Edith Turner. The sheriff's wife, whom Ms. Agnes had pointed out at the funeral.

Something about Edith made Kate's skin tingle. And not in a good way.

"Let's go, Heather." Kate nudged the teen from her chair. "We should get home before your dad does. I wouldn't want him to worry."

Kate wasn't as concerned about Nolan as she was about the woman who continued to stare at them until they left the coffee shop.

Nolan heard the car and peered out the window just as the red two-door pulled into the garage.

He let out a sigh of relief. Heather and Kate were home, at last.

Thank you, Lord.

Heather stepped from the garage, a book in one hand, the other on Kate's elbow, helping her with her crutch. Together, they made their way toward the house.

The back door creaked open. Kate and Heather entered the kitchen oblivious to the panic their absence had caused him.

"Hey, Dad." Heather's eyes twinkled, her cheeks rosy from the cold. Kate smiled as if she was glad to see him.

Earlier, walking into an empty house had sent him into turmoil. Talk about worst-case scenario. When he'd heard the sirens, the thoughts that had rambled through his mind had made his heart pound in terror — an accident, ambulances, another bizarre incident taking someone he loved.

Now, all the fear he had tried to hold in check broke loose.

"Where have you two been?" he demanded, hearing the worry in his voice.

Heather glanced at Kate before turning back to her father. "We were —"

"Heather forgot a book at school," Kate volunteered. She scooted forward, positioning herself between Nolan and his daughter.

Did Kate think she needed to protect Heather? Now, that annoyed him.

"I'm talking to Heather," Nolan said, remaining outwardly calm. Inside, he was tied in knots. He couldn't get past the terror of thinking Heather and Kate had been involved in an accident.

"Yes, but —"

"But nothing, Kate," he said slowly. "My daughter has a voice. She can answer for herself."

The woman's eyes grew wide. She pulled in a deep breath, her nostrils flared. "You're upset, Nolan."

"That's right. Upset *and* worried. I didn't know where either of you were."

Heather peered around Kate's shoulder and held up a textbook. "I forgot my math book at school, Dad. Kate said we could go back to get it. Then we stopped for coffee."

His eyes dropped to Kate's injured leg. "You drove?"

Kate sighed and raked a hand through her hair. "Actually —"

"*I* drove, Dad." Heather stepped around Kate. "Remember I've got my learner's. It's okay. We didn't have any problems."

"Why didn't you ask my permission?"

Heather clutched the book to her chest. "I called your cell."

"But you didn't leave a message."

"Well, I . . ." She glanced from Nolan to Kate and to Nolan again. "I thought you'd see the missed call."

"You didn't leave a message because you knew I'd say no."

"Dad!"

Nolan let out a frustrated breath. "Go to your room, Heather. We'll discuss this later."

"But, Dad," she whined.

"No buts. Do as I say, young lady."

Textbook in hand, Heather stomped out of the kitchen.

Kate stood staring at him, as if *he'd* done something wrong.

Stupid, really, to allow his emotions to get out of control. But there had been too many accidents. Too many fatalities.

Kate didn't know he had followed the sirens to the ravine and the sheer terror he'd felt as he'd looked fifteen feet down at the broken body of a girl not much older than Heather.

She didn't need to hear the gruesome details. Plus, she'd probably want to add her two cents.

She always had an opinion that invariably differed from his, especially when it involved Heather. Of course, Kate didn't have children, didn't seem to even have friends from the absence of phone calls to and from Atlanta.

The way he felt right now, neither he nor his daughter needed Kate Murphy in their lives. Let her hightail it back to Atlanta.

The sooner Kate left Mercy the better.

Then, he looked into her blue eyes and realized the only person he was trying to fool was himself.

TWELVE

Kate stood alone in the middle of the kitchen. The door to the basement slammed as Nolan charged down the steps, his heavy footsteps resounding through the house.

Overhead, the door to Heather's room swung shut.

This family had a lot of problems. Lack of communication ranked at the top of the list.

Kate understood why Nolan was upset. Coming home to an empty house had frightened him. Especially after losing his wife.

As Heather had said earlier that afternoon, when families lost a loved one, they held on tighter than they should to those left behind.

Although right now, the teen couldn't see beyond her dad's anger. Wouldn't take much for Heather to stop making the effort to open the lines of communication if the door kept closing in her face.

Kate knew that firsthand. As well as the

long-term repercussions.

The less-than-perfect relationship she had with her own dad had carried over into her adult life. Despite her grandfather's determination to surround Kate with love, she had remained guarded with relationships and hesitant to accept a helping hand.

She didn't want Heather to be burdened with problems later in life because she couldn't have an open dialogue with her dad at this critical time.

Kate could tell Nolan a thing or two about how he needed to tune in to his daughter. But would he listen?

Probably not, although that hadn't stopped her before.

Tucking a crutch under her arm, Kate headed for the basement. Not that she felt up to navigating another set of stairs with her wobbly leg. Chances were Nolan might not want her advice, but it needed to be said.

Descending the steep steps took even more effort than she'd realized. By the time she reached the bottom landing, her arms ached and her good leg threatened to buckle with fatigue.

A long hallway led to a door that hung partially open. As quietly as possible, she eased forward.

Peering inside the room, she saw Nolan seated behind a desk, eyes closed, hands together, fingers steepled. A Bible lay open before him.

Talk about bad timing.

She'd wait until he finished his talk with the Lord. Kate glanced around the room. Top-of-the-line computer. Floor-to-ceiling bookcases. An assortment of hardbacks sat neatly arranged on the shelves, interspersed with photos of Heather and Olivia. Smiling faces attesting to the way life had been.

Too private. Kate needed to backtrack. Starting to turn away, she noticed a painting of a stormy sky hanging on the far wall. What caught her attention were the rays of light breaking through the dark clouds.

Warmth spread through her body.

Grandda had carried a similar picture in his Bible of light cutting through a dark and ominous sky.

"A God sky," he had called it. She could still hear his voice. *"That light shows the unconditional love and mercy Christ constantly showers down upon us, Katie-girl."*

Kate began to tremble. She closed her eyes, struggling to hold her emotions in check as the memory of the love of the Lord she had once known played through her mind.

All her life, she'd tried to be the perfect daughter to her earthly father as well as her heavenly one. Only she'd failed on both counts. Just as she'd failed with Eddie and Tina, with her research at Bannister Scientific, with her attempt to reconcile Nolan and his daughter.

Better to leave Nolan to his prayers than to fail again. Kate pivoted. Her crutch caught on the rug. She tripped and gasped with pain as her shoulder crashed into the door frame.

Just as quickly, Nolan's strong arms caught her and pulled her upright.

"Kate?" Concern crossed his raised brow. "How'd you get down here?"

She looked deep into his eyes. A sense of security swept over her. The man always appeared when she was most in need.

Mentally, she shook off the thought. Pulling a wall of self-sufficiency up around her fragile heart, she backed out of his grasp. "I walked, Nolan. I'm not as handicapped as I look."

He dropped his hands and frowned as if her words had cut him like a knife.

"Look, I'm probably making a fool of myself by always adding my opinion, but I thought we should talk."

"About . . . ?"

About the flawed way you deal with your daughter, Kate wanted to say. But she bit her tongue. Honey instead of vinegar. "About Heather."

A wary glint flashed in Nolan's eyes.

"I'm speaking as a friend," Kate continued, although she knew she was stretching the point. They'd met only three days ago. Seemed longer.

He held up his hands. "I overreacted upstairs. It's just that . . ." He hesitated. "I didn't know what had happened to either of you."

"I understand how you'd be upset, but Heather's a good driver. You should be proud of her."

"I am proud. Her driving's not the problem. It's the mountain roads and the other drivers. Since we moved here, a number of people have died in tragic crashes. Two of them were teenagers."

Kate gasped. "Friends of Heather's?"

He shook his head. "Older kids. She'd seen them around school, but didn't know them. Still, for a parent . . ." He turned his head and looked at a picture of his daughter on the far wall.

"When I got home today, I heard sirens. My mind went wild, thinking it was Heather. That you were with her. I called the sheriff's office. They couldn't or wouldn't tell me anything over the phone, so I got back in my car and headed to the crash. Turns out it was a young woman, about twenty-one."

Kate saw the fear that had, no doubt, overwhelmed him earlier. "Oh, Nolan. I'm so sorry. A drive to school seemed harmless at the time. And I thought Heather had left you a voice mail. The last thing you need is more on your shoulders when you're already carrying such a heavy load, making a new life for yourself and your daughter."

"Not the best idea to pluck a teen out of her established environment. Most days, I think we should have stayed in California."

"But Heather likes it here in Mercy."

Surprise washed over his face. "She told you that?"

Kate nodded. "Just this afternoon, when we were in the car. Let a kid get behind the wheel and suddenly the barriers come tumbling down. She said she'd felt like an outsider with the kids in L.A. Guess they all had big bank accounts and lived life in the fast lane."

Nolan rested an arm on the doorjamb and hung his head. "And all this time, I thought Heather wanted to go back."

"She said the kids are nice here. They

included her right away. The only problem is you."

He jerked his head up. "Me?"

"You're too restrictive."

"She's a child, Kate."

"But with a good head on her shoulders. When was the last time you had a conversation with her like an equal?"

He pointed a finger at his chest. "I'm her father, not her peer."

"Have you two ever talked about Jimmy Ramos?"

"The kid from the funeral?"

"The one you evidently didn't want hanging around the other day. I met him at the coffee shop. He seems nice."

"The boy's parents died a few years ago. His older brother's raising him."

"And that's a problem?" Kate asked. Or was something else bothering Nolan? "Is it because he's Hispanic?"

Nolan bristled. "For goodness' sake, Kate. How could you think that of me? His ethnicity has nothing to do with my feelings. I'm just not ready for Heather to be involved with *any* boy."

"She told me Jimmy helps out with an after-school program at the elementary school."

"And he tutors kids with their math. I've

heard all that. It's just . . ." Nolan hesitated.

"Your little girl's growing up and you're having a hard time letting go."

"She's too young to date," he insisted.

"Maybe, but what about supervised group outings?"

"Heather's fifteen."

"That's exactly my point," Kate said. "Friends are important in the teen years. You need to know her friends to ensure they're good kids. You've got to talk to her on her terms. Keep the door open, even when it's late or you're tired or you've got a business trip in the morning."

Nolan stared down at her. "How did you become such an expert on teens?"

Kate thought for a moment. "Heather reminds me of myself. I guess I still remember what I needed at that age. I lived in the present. Tomorrow seemed an eternity away. That's why you have to talk to her every day, Nolan. Find out what and who is important to her. You might be pleasantly surprised."

"Heather and I are doing okay."

"In whose opinion?" Kate glanced at the rays of light in the painting on the wall. "You told me about God's unconditional love. Don't you believe in it yourself?"

"Of course I do."

"God loves Heather even more than you do. Ask the Lord to protect her."

"I have," Nolan confessed. "But I'm still worried." He shook his head. "Maybe I don't trust Him enough."

"Then work on it," Kate said. "Start by opening your home to your daughter's friends. It might help you open your heart, as well."

Nolan almost choked. *My heart?*

Kate didn't have a clue. Probably a good thing. No reason for her to know that his heart felt raw and exposed whenever he got close to her.

He'd always been a calm, logical person. These last few days since Kate had dropped into his life, he hadn't been acting like himself.

"So if you let me drive Tina's car . . ."

What was she saying now? Nolan shook his head ever so slightly and tried to focus.

"Tina's car," she repeated, probably noting the rather lost look he'd given her. "If you'll let me drive Tina's car to Atlanta."

He blinked. Was she leaving?

"Whenever the garage is finished working on my car, I'll drive back to Mercy for an exchange."

She was leaving.

"Nolan, did you hear me?"

He nodded. "Yeah, sure. Tina's car? The problem's the spare tire. That's why I got upset when Heather said you two were driving around town. The spare's not made for long-distance travel."

"Then I'll stop by the garage on the way out of town and have the spare replaced with a new tire."

So she *was* leaving.

"Is that all right with you, Nolan?"

"Ah . . ." No, it wasn't all right. He wanted her to stay. "Why so soon?"

She sighed. "Didn't I tell you I planned to leave on Tuesday?"

"No, you didn't. I thought you'd be here a little longer." He let out a deep breath. "If you have to go, talk to Hank at the garage about the tire and charge it to my account."

She shook her head emphatically. "I don't need your money."

What did that mean?

"No doubt, Tracy Farrington's grateful for the help you're giving her. And I'm sure Tina appreciated the bonus."

Now Nolan was the one who didn't have a clue. "Bonus?"

"The check for five thousand dollars. I saw it in Tina's desk drawer."

The realization of what Kate had just

divulged spread over her face. She held up her hands in defense. "Honestly, I wasn't snooping. I was looking for my cross."

Suddenly, he understood. Injured leg, could barely hobble from the bedroom to the kitchen, yet she was climbing steep stairs in the garage. The woman amazed him.

Nolan reached out a hand and touched her shoulder. "Relax, Kate. You and Tina were friends. You can look around all you want."

Her defensive edge softened, and his heart went out to her. "Tina didn't have any cash in reserve," he explained. "Her mom's funeral used up her savings and didn't cover a marble headstone."

"So she was leaving Mercy?"

"Just for a few weeks," he said. "Tracy was going to fill in while Tina was gone."

"And you gave Tina the money to cover the cost of the headstone?"

His lips broke into a smile. "Tina was stubborn. Just like you. She called it a loan and wanted to work out some type of payment plan before she cashed the check."

Kate sighed. "I'm sorry, Nolan. I haven't been myself recently. Seems I keep jumping to the wrong conclusions."

"You were in a serious accident, Kate. Then you learned your good friend had died. And the only place you could find shelter was in the home of a strange man and his teenage daughter."

"And to think all this happened because I wanted to find my cross."

Nolan tilted his head and stared down at her. "There's something I've been meaning to ask you, Kate. If God doesn't have a high priority in your life, why's the cross so important? Didn't you give it to Tina?"

Kate hitched in a breath. "I gave it to her brother."

Nolan saw the heartache wash over her face. He softened his voice as everything fell into place. "You loved him, didn't you?"

"I thought I loved him, only he was a fraud, a manipulator." She looked fleetingly at the painting hanging on the wall before she turned her gaze back on him. "You're right, Nolan. I don't have much use for God. And unlike you, I struggle with the whole idea of His unconditional love."

Nolan touched her cheek. "Human love is a choice, Kate. But God's love is freely given and knows no bounds."

She looked into his eyes, and he saw her soulful struggle to accept Christ back into her life. For an instant, her firm resolve seemed to falter. Then she shoved it back in place.

"I'll leave in the morning," Kate said. "After Heather goes to school. I want to say goodbye to her first. And if you ever find my cross, mail it to me."

Without giving him time to comment, Kate turned and hobbled out of his office. He wanted to rush after her and beg her to stay. But Kate needed to move on with her life, a life that didn't include him.

Let her go, his voice of reason warned. No need for her to hang around Mercy. When he got the evidence he needed, he and Heather would be leaving, as well.

But Heather liked it here?

Now that surprised him. Maybe he didn't have all the answers. He'd have a long chat with his daughter. See if there were other secrets she kept buried in her heart.

He shook his head.

Lord, help me.

If he lost Heather, he'd lose it all.

A heavy weight settled on his shoulders. No matter how hard he tried to deny his feelings, over the last three days, Kate had found a spot in his heart, as well. Would he lose her along with Heather?

THIRTEEN

Kate struggled up the stairs to the main floor after leaving Nolan's office. Her eyes burned hot with tears she tried to keep in check. She had cried too much in the last few days.

At least she was going back to Atlanta. Better to hole up in her lonely apartment than to struggle with her fickle emotions here in Mercy.

Three years ago, she'd closed her heart and vowed to never allow another man entry. Nolan Price had come closer than anyone to breaking down her resistance. If she stayed much longer, her resolve would crumble.

Squaring her shoulders, she stepped into the hallway and shuffled to the guest room. The light from the bedside lamp welcomed her as she pulled the door closed behind her, scooted to the bed and collapsed onto the crisp cotton comforter.

Her tears broke free. Kate grabbed the quilt folded over the bottom of the bed and pulled it around her shoulders. What was wrong with her?

As much as she wanted to be strong, her heart ached with longing for the security of a home, a child, a man to love and to love her in return.

Kate swiped her hand over her face, hoping to chase away her tears and her foolish thoughts. First thing in the morning, she'd leave Mercy and head back to Atlanta where she could forget about what might have been.

Nolan unlocked the bottom drawer of his file cabinet, withdrew an unmarked manila folder and dropped it onto his desk. Photos stared back at him. Photos Nolan had secretly taken under the cover of darkness. Photos of the bodies of accident victims being whisked out of Mercy MedClinic and loaded into the back of Wade Green's transport van.

In each shot, Doc Samuels stood watch as Wade pushed a draped gurney across the delivery platform to the waiting vehicle.

The remains left the clinic in the middle of the night when no one was around to witness the transport or examine the bodies. Official autopsies didn't require clandestine measures.

What was going on?

Olivia had said the clinic where she'd received the special pretransplant treatment had been secluded in a densely forested area. If Lloyd's special treatment hadn't undergone clinical trials and FDA approval, he wouldn't want people happening upon the secret medical facility. But would he stoop to murder to protect his role in the transplant tourist operation?

Nolan wouldn't put anything past the doc, and his paying for the cremation of Mercy's accident victims was further circumstantial evidence.

Nolan sighed. Nothing could be proven from any of the photos he'd taken so far except that Wade and the doc worked at night. Nolan needed concrete evidence of any wrongdoing.

Tina had left a voice mail saying she'd seen something in the woods. Had she found the secluded clinic? Was that the reason Marty Jackson and the other accident victims had died, as well?

Nolan withdrew his camera from the bottom desk drawer and adjusted the settings for night photography.

Tonight, he would wait outside the clinic.

If the body of today's young accident victim was removed, he'd document the transport. With a lot of luck, he might be able to learn the truth about what was happening in Mercy. If Lloyd's nocturnal operation provided a link to the Beverly Hills operation, the end might be in sight.

As long as everything went as planned tonight.

Kate crawled into bed, pulled the comforter to her chest and opened the journal. Growing up in El Paso, she and Tina had shared everything — their struggles with school, their growing interest in boys, as well as their dreams for the future.

Tina had yearned for stardom. Hollywood, the big screen, a chance for fame and fortune. Kate had hoped to find a cure for diabetes to save her grandfather and others from the terrible complications of the disease.

While neither of them had achieved their goals, Tina had developed a strong relationship with the Lord. Plus, she had found a family who needed her and a teenage girl who loved her.

Kate's advanced degree in chemistry paled in comparison.

Tina had chosen the better portion, after all.

Kate flipped the book to the last page and read the entry Tina had scribbled the night before she'd died.

I found something in the woods and plan to tell Nolan tomorrow, although I doubt he'll know what to make of it, either. If only I could talk to someone with a medical or scientific background. I keep thinking of Kate.

Has the Lord placed her name on my heart?

How deeply I regret the mistake I made three years ago when I turned my back on her. I should have believed Kate when she told me about Eddie.

Oh, Lord, I beg your forgiveness. I was blinded by grief and not able to accept the truth. Unfortunately, I lost a dear friend because of it.

Should I call her? After all this time, would she give me a second chance?

I know Kate. She'd forgive me. In fact, she'd probably open her arms like the father in the prodigal son story. Kate's a good woman with a big heart, and her love is unconditional.

How could Tina think so highly of her? And come to such a wrong conclusion?

Kate's heart had hardened into granite. She couldn't forgive. Worse than that, she couldn't love.

In her mind's eye, Kate pictured Nolan, smiling down at her.

She shook her head. Usually, she acted like a rational adult. Around Nolan, she blurted out the most irrational things she later regretted.

As she ran her finger over Tina's bold script, a sense of loss overwhelmed Kate once again. If only Tina had lived. Maybe she could have taught Kate how to forgive.

And Nolan?

If Tina were still alive, Kate might have learned how to love, as well.

Kate straightened the comforter, determined to push the thoughts from her mind. She needed to focus on Tina, a woman who had loved God and understood what was important in life.

If the Lord loved Tina, could He love Kate? Doubtful. And yet . . .

Kate flipped to another entry. The more she read, the more convinced she was of Tina's commitment to helping others. In a number of places, she mentioned visiting Sue Ann and the bond that had formed between them.

While Tina had noticed signs of dementia

in Agnes, she'd been more concerned with the paraplegic's depression and growing sense of paranoia. Tina had prayed with and for Sue Ann on a regular basis, asking the Lord to bring hope and peace to Sue Ann's troubled heart.

Eventually, Kate's eyes grew heavy, and she drifted to sleep, the journal still on her chest.

A noise woke her sometime later. She opened her eyes as Nolan's heavy footsteps descended the stairs, entered the kitchen and walked across the tile floor. The back door creaked open. Then closed.

Kate rose from the bed and watched from the window as his SUV left the driveway and headed toward town.

She glanced at the clock on the nightstand — 1:00 a.m.

Where was Nolan going in the middle of the night?

Wind howled through the trees as Nolan pulled into the rear employee parking lot at Mercy MedClinic. The night hung as dark as pitch outside his car window. A lone light illuminated the delivery platform, sending long shadows to play over the garbage Dumpsters positioned on the pavement below.

Nolan hunkered down in the driver's seat, his eyes peeled for Wade Green's transport van. At 2:00 a.m., an engine sounded in the distance.

Reaching for his camera, Nolan watched the white van back up to the platform. The driver's door opened, and the funeral director, dressed in jeans and a flannel jacket, jumped to the pavement, rounded the vehicle and climbed the seven steps to the MedClinic's service door. He paused long enough to glance around the lot before he scurried inside.

Nolan snapped three shots of the fleeting figure, then checked the photos. Even using his zoom lens, he was too far away to get a clear picture. He needed to move closer.

Carefully, Nolan inched open the driver's door and slipped from the SUV. Dressed in black, he hoped to blend in with the surrounding parked cars as he made his way through the lot. When he was no more than ten feet from the Dumpsters, the clinic door swung open.

Nolan dropped to his knees and peered around the bumper of a blue minivan. Wade Green stood on the platform and studied the windy night before he reentered the building.

Nolan dashed toward the Dumpsters and

breathed a sigh of relief when he slipped into their dark shadow. Hidden from view, he raised his camera and waited until the door opened once again.

Wade pushed a draped gurney into the night. Doc Samuels followed, condensation from his breath clouding the air as he spoke.

"Take it easy with her, Wade. And don't give me any more of that nonsense."

"Like I told you, Doc, I want out."

Samuels laughed softly. "You're talking crazy."

"Janelle and I are leaving Mercy."

"And how will you afford Janelle's medication? You know her back pain requires expensive prescription drugs."

"I can start over in another town."

"Don't make me laugh, Wade. Janelle would never leave. Besides, I pay you more than you could ever make in *any* funeral business."

"I've had enough killing."

"Accidents, Wade."

"Call them what you like, but you lied to me. You said you were dealing with a scientific breakthrough that would help thousands."

"I am."

"Get real, Doc. Twenty-one-year-old girls weren't part of the plan."

Nolan raised his camera. Click. Click. Click.

Wade pushed the gurney toward the van. Wind swirled through the branches of the trees overhead.

A strong gust blew across the pavement, picked up dust and debris, then whirled through the air.

"What the —" Wade jerked his arm up to cover his face from the flying particles. His hand caught on the drape. The cloth flew back, exposing the ashen face of the young accident victim Nolan had seen at the bottom of the deep ravine.

Click. Click. Click.

Wade slid the body into the van, slammed the door and waved his hand in the air as he climbed into the driver's seat. "We'll settle this later, Doc."

Samuels hurried back into the clinic.

Nolan checked the digital photos. The face of the young woman was clearly visible on the screen.

Seconds later, the doc stepped outside. Before Nolan could reach his SUV, Samuels had climbed into his car and raced off into the darkness.

Nolan wouldn't be able to follow Lloyd tonight, but at least he had photos of the young woman.

If only he could see the full picture of what was happening in Mercy.

Fourteen

Glancing in the mirror the next morning, Kate noticed the bags under her eyes, a visual reminder she'd stayed awake too long after Nolan had left the house. Around 2:00 a.m., she had finished reading Tina's diary and had fallen back asleep. Nolan still hadn't returned home.

Kate had expected to find inconsistencies in Tina's entries. Surely, the real Tina couldn't be as focused on Christ as everyone thought. But the journal revealed just the opposite. Tina had been on fire with love for the Lord.

And what had that gotten her?

An early death on the side of an isolated farm road.

Tina had written about her skin rash growing worse. Dr. Samuels had prescribed a special cream that had failed to improve the condition. Tina was beginning to think she needed to see a specialist.

Before reading the journal, Kate's scientific mind had worked overtime, questioning Tina's death. But Kate had ignored one simple fact. Often the most obvious answer was the right one.

Tina *did* have a skin condition that had grown progressively worse. No reason why the rash couldn't have been latex induced or that changing the tire hadn't triggered an anaphylactic reaction.

Let Tina rest in peace.

Time for Kate to head back to Atlanta, back to a lonely apartment and nine more days until she'd find out if she still had a job.

Kate opened her bedroom door as Heather stepped into the hallway, schoolbooks in hand.

"I left something for you on the table." The girl pointed back to the kitchen door she'd just exited. "Something I made for Tina on her last birthday. I've had it in my room since Friday. It helped me." Heather dropped her eyes. "With the pain and all."

The teen pulled in a deep breath before she raised her gaze. "After yesterday, I knew we were friends. I wanted to share it with you."

Heather's sincerity touched Kate. Evidently, their afternoon together had been as meaningful to Heather as it had been to Kate.

"Tina helped me pick out this outfit." Heather twirled around, showing off the teal sweater and black skirt. "We went shopping the day after her birthday. Dad had given Tina some money, and we both decided to buy something new."

More money from Nolan.

"Wearing it reminds me of her, but in a good way, you know what I mean?"

Kate did know. Memories could heal a broken heart, memories of love and commitment. Not memories of betrayal.

"Can we go for another ride when I get home from school?"

Kate hesitated. Heaviness filled her heart. "Heather, I have to go back to Atlanta today."

"You're leaving?" Confusion clouded the girl's face. "But why?"

"I have a job."

Heather blinked as tears filled her eyes. "But your leg? You need to get better first."

"I've been enough trouble for you and your dad."

"Trouble?" Heather shook her head and stepped toward the front door and away from Kate. Pain flashed in her eyes. "I thought we were friends."

"We are. I'll be back to pick up my car in a week or two. We'll do something then."

"Don't bother." Heather clutched her books closer to her chest, grabbed her coat and charged out of the house, slamming the door behind her.

Kate's heart ached. What had she done?

Death had taken Olivia and Tina. Now, Kate was walking out of Heather's life, as well.

Nolan preached about God's unconditional love. Empty rhetoric. A loving God would listen to a teen's broken heart. God didn't love unconditionally. Times like this, Kate wondered if He loved at all.

In the kitchen, Nolan slammed a cabinet door.

Seemed everyone was having a bad day.

Maybe she *should* stay one more night. If Nolan agreed, Heather could practice her driving while she and Kate discussed dads who didn't understand their daughters. Another evening together to shore up their fledgling friendship.

They could make plans for Heather to visit Kate in the not-too-distant future. In Atlanta, they could go shopping, tour the Aquarium, maybe see a play at the Fox.

Kate pushed open the door to the kitchen. Nolan stood at the counter with a bagel raised halfway to his open mouth. The bags under his eyes looked even more pronounced than Kate's. From all appearances, his late-night excursion had taken a toll.

"Morning," she said as she shuffled to the coffeepot and poured herself a cup.

Nolan had a lot to learn about his daughter, but at least he'd listened last night. She needed to cut the man a little slack. She was too hard on people.

Her grandfather had pointed that out to her in his not-so-tactful way. *"People aren't perfect, Katie-girl. They make mistakes. A little tolerance and understanding goes a long way."*

Grandda was right, of course.

"Listen, I'm sorry about last night," Kate said. "I got carried away. I'll stay a few more days. Heather and I —"

Nolan dropped the rest of the bagel onto his plate. "Wouldn't want to upset your schedule. I called Tracy Farrington. She's coming over this morning."

"Tracy?"

"She'll stay with Heather. Be sure to get the tire changed before you head back to Atlanta. I'll call you when your car's ready."

"But —" She didn't want to leave.

Nolan grabbed his briefcase and overcoat. "Thanks for all your help, Kate."

He turned his back on her and strode out the door. Kate watched him walk away as she stood alone in the now lonely house.

Another mistake on her part. She'd made so many. She was the one who needed advice on relationships.

Wrapping her arms around her waist, she moaned. What was wrong with her? Why did she demand so much from people? Did she really expect them to be perfect?

A photo album lay on the kitchen table along with a note addressed to Kate that was propped against a small cardboard box.

Recognizing Heather's youthful script, Kate tore opened the envelope.

Dear Kate,

I know you came to Mercy to find your grandfather's cross. Tina showed it to me a long time ago. She said it belonged to her dearest friend, and she hoped to give it back one day. After Tina died and you arrived at our house, I didn't want to part with anything Tina had, so I went to her apartment and took the cross. But now, I know you should have it. I also know you'll understand and not get mad at me for keeping it from you. Tina said you were always so forgiving.

Your friend, Heather.

A lump formed in Kate's throat. Her hands shook as she opened the box and pulled out the gold cross that had been missing from her life for over three years.

Grandda's cross.

She fingered the heavy Florentine metal and slipped the chain over her head. A sense of security settled over her as comforting as her grandfather's warm embrace.

She touched the corner of the album and flipped open the book. A photo of Tina smiled back at her.

The next page held a picture of Tina and Heather with arms entwined. Their smiles and the happiness reflected in the deep bond the two had shared cut through Kate's wall of isolation.

Easier to run away than to face the promise of what could be. A friendship with Heather that could stretch into the future.

And what about Nolan?

The feelings that tugged on her heart whenever he was around frightened her. Eddie had betrayed her. Her father had walked out of her life. Would Nolan hurt her, as well? She was too much of a coward to find out.

She flipped to another page and then another. Love poured forth from the faces in the photos and touched her broken heart. Tears rolled down her cheeks.

She and Tina had pledged to be friends for life. Of the two of them, Tina was the good one, the one who deserved to live. She had been so well loved in this home while Kate seemed to have constantly disrupted the status quo.

Kate turned the page and stopped cold.

The photo showed Tina standing under a vinyl banner that read Happy 29th Birthday. In front of her, a large birthday cake sat ablaze with candles while at least a dozen balloons floated around her. Large helium-filled balloons.

Balloons made of latex.

If Tina's sensitivity was as acute as Dr. Samuels had said, Tina would have been in desperate trouble with such a large exposure.

But Heather had said she and Tina had gone shopping the next day. Tina hadn't gotten sick nor had she experienced an allergic reaction.

Latex hadn't killed Tina. Someone was lying. But who? Dr. Samuels? The funeral director?

Or Nolan Price?

Nolan glanced at his watch just before he

turned onto the main road and accelerated. He wanted to arrive at the airport before the first morning flight from LAX landed. Any other time and he would have offered Kate a ride to Atlanta. But today he couldn't risk her asking questions about the reason for his trip.

Nolan's phone vibrated. One hand on the steering wheel, he grabbed the cell with his other. "Price."

"It's Hank, sir. Tracy said you called this morning when I was in the shower. Pauline was able to access those computer files yesterday."

"Just so she covered her tracks. I don't want to put her in danger." Too many women had died already.

"She said no one would know she'd copied the photos."

"How many were there?"

"Marty Jackson, of course. Plus, those kids who crashed a while back on the Summerton pass. And two others." Hank paused. "You'll recognize one of them, for sure. Pauline saved the photos to a disk and made a hard copy. I put them in an envelope and asked Tracy to give it to you as soon as you get home."

"Thanks, Hank. I'm grateful for Pauline's help."

Nolan flipped the phone shut. Why was Wade keeping the photos on his computer? Was he documenting the deaths for his own purposes? The funeral director had told Dr. Samuels he wanted out. Perhaps the photos would provide evidence he would hold over Lloyd's head at a later time.

Nolan sighed. Hank claimed the accidents had been rigged. Had the victims stumbled onto the secluded clinic? Was that the reason they lost their lives?

No matter the reason, one thing was certain. Lloyd was involved in the deaths of at least five people in Mercy.

But who was in charge? Would the trail of corruption lead back to the Beverly Hills physicians?

As Nolan drove to Atlanta, he tried to piece the parts of the puzzle together. Soon, other thoughts played through his mind. Thoughts of a houseguest who made his heart pound and his pulse race.

Why had Kate Murphy slammed into the creek and into his life when he was so close to finding the evidence he needed? She had turned his world upside down, and now she was heading back to Atlanta.

No doubt for the best. He'd be free of the distraction she caused in his life.

He needed to stay focused on what was

happening in Mercy. Not on Kate Murphy. Nolan sighed. Easier said than done.

FIFTEEN

The buzzer rang twice before Kate could grab her crutch and open the front door. Tracy Farrington stood on the steps, wearing a navy jacket and a jersey sweat suit stretched over a protruding and very pregnant belly.

With her red hair pulled back in a ponytail, the woman's face appeared swollen, but her eyes were clear and her smile warm as she greeted Kate.

"Sorry I'm late." Tracy turned and waved at the car backing out of the driveway. "Like I told you over the phone, my brother-in-law couldn't drop me off until now. Hank's driving over to Caldwell. Ray wants him to pick up a couple of auto parts."

Tracy stepped into the house and closed the door behind her, then paused for a second and rubbed her left hand over her tummy.

"Are you feeling okay?" Kate asked.

"Sure. Baby's fine. I'm fine. And we're into the countdown. Two weeks." Tracy held up the tote she carried in her right hand. "I packed light. Hank said he'd bring more of my things over tomorrow morning."

Kate reached for the bag. "I'll take this."

Tracy shook her head. "Looks like you've got more problems walking than I do. Just point me in the right direction. Guest room's down the hall, isn't it?"

Kate hadn't finished packing. Maybe she'd been hoping Tracy would be a no-show. "I changed the sheets earlier, but give me a few minutes to pull my things together."

"Don't let me rush you," Tracy said.

"You're not. I just got busy this morning, and the time passed too quickly."

Fact was she'd spent most of the morning on the Internet, trying to learn more about the transplant tourist industry.

"Listen, I drank a bottle of water on the way over here, and I'm about ready to burst. Bathroom is —" Tracy held out her hands and shrugged her shoulders. "Where?"

"Straight down the hall." Kate pointed to the first door past the kitchen.

"Be out in a flash. Then you can give me a tour and tell me what I need to know. Nolan's a basket case when it comes to that daughter of his. It's a wonder he didn't leave me a list of instructions."

Kate smiled. "Sounds like something Nolan would do."

"Guess if my wife had died and I was trying to raise an independent fifteen-year-old, I might be overprotective, as well. Still?" She flipped her ponytail. "Heather's got to have a life, you know what I mean?"

Tracy continued to talk as she headed down the hall. "Like I told my sister, you have a kid, you have to expect them to grow up."

"How about a cup of tea?" Kate called after her.

Tracy glanced over her shoulder. "No, thanks, but you go ahead."

Kate ducked into the guest room and quickly tucked a few items into the plastic bag filled with the clothing Pauline had laundered.

Opening the nightstand drawer, Kate stared for a long moment at Tina's journal. Should she return the book to Tina's apartment? Doubtful Nolan even knew the book existed, and she didn't have the time or the energy to climb the garage steps again. She shoved the journal into the plastic bag and hauled it into the foyer.

Continuing on to the kitchen, Kate placed

the tea kettle on the burner before she peeked into the alcove where the photo of Olivia sat next to the computer.

What was it about Olivia's death that bothered her?

The kettle whistled. Kate poured water over the teabag, took a sip of the hot brew and looked up when Tracy stuck her head in the kitchen.

"Mind if I lie down for a few minutes before that tour? I feel a little light-headed."

"You're not getting sick, are you?"

"I'm just tired. It's probably the pregnancy. Will I keep you from packing?"

"I've got everything. Besides, I should probably call my boss in Atlanta and let him know I'm heading back to town. Rest for a while, then I'll show you around the house."

As Tracy padded back to the bedroom, Kate stared at the phone.

Once again she thought of Olivia and shook her head. Why couldn't she let the whole thing go? She was ready to leave Mercy, but something kept niggling her about Olivia's death.

What had Jason mentioned a few months ago? For the life of her, she couldn't remember.

A good reason to swallow her pride and

check in with Bannister Scientific. Too soon for the review board to make a decision, but Kate wanted Jason to know she'd be ready to return to work if and when he needed her.

Kate dialed the toll-free number.

"Marge, it's Kate," she said once Jason's secretary got on the line. "Jason's probably tied up with the board, but I wanted to let you know I've been out of town for the last few days."

"Oh, my gosh, Kate, it's good to hear your voice. I've been calling your condo. Jason wants to talk to you."

An overpowering sense of dread swept over Kate. More bad news?

"Hold on while I put you through."

Kate glanced out the window. Dark clouds gathered in the distance. About as dark as her mood had suddenly turned.

Nothing pleasant about waiting to hear Jason explain how her services were no longer needed at Bannister. For the good of the company, of course, he'd probably add to soften the blow.

No job. An old friend dead, Grandda, Mrs. Espinosa, Eddie — everyone she had loved once upon a time gone.

Where would that leave her? All alone.

So why had she turned her back on Nolan

and Heather, the two people who were starting to occupy a place in her heart?

"Kate!" Jason's voice filled the line. "Glad you checked in. I wanted to make sure you understood about this two-week hold on your research. Marge tried to reach you at your condo, but no answer. Where are you?"

"In North Georgia. I'm staying with a family in Mercy." She thought of Nolan's surprise when she'd told him she was leaving and Heather's tear-filled eyes as she'd run to catch the school bus. "How's the deliberation going?"

"Still up in the air. That article in the newspaper is the main hurdle."

"I was misquoted, and you know it, Jason."

"That's the reason I didn't want you to do the interview in the first place, Kate. The merger is a hot issue. You put Bannister Scientific in a difficult position."

"The reporter told me I'd be able to review the article before it went to press."

"Believing him was a mistake. Wish I could give you a more positive outlook, but the board didn't appreciate having the company's name make the front page."

"I told the truth, Jason."

"Yes, but sometimes the truth is hard to accept, especially when the reporter slants the story. Right now, the board's in a deadlock."

"What about my documentation? I outlined what I found in my report."

"They haven't had time to review your papers. I'll have Marge make sure they get copies of your report. Maybe it will help. But I can't promise anything."

"I'll be back in Atlanta this evening. Let me know when they make a decision."

"Will do. Glad you got a little relaxation over the long weekend."

"Hardly. An old friend passed away. I attended her funeral."

"Oh, Kate. I'm sorry."

She explained about Tina's so-called allergy to latex that didn't add up, especially after seeing the photo of her surrounded by helium-filled balloons.

"Sounds like your friend should have gotten a second opinion," Jason said.

"No chance in this town. Only one physician, and from what I've seen, Lloyd Samuels doesn't like his authority questioned."

"Birthmark over his left eyebrow?"

"You know him?"

"No, but he presented a paper at a conference I attended years ago. The research community is a tight-knit group. Some people are hard to forget. I never expected

Dr. Samuels would end up in Georgia."

"How's that?"

"Last time I heard, he was collaborating with a West Coast physician." Jason paused. "Can't recall the guy's name, but they worked together for a number of years. There was a rumor that Dr. Samuels had gotten into a little trouble, and the collaboration ended."

"What kind of trouble, Jason?"

"The way I heard it, he's manic-depressive. When he takes his meds he's okay. Otherwise, he has this inflated-ego problem. The guy's a genius, just not real levelheaded."

Ego or not, Kate wanted to have a talk with Doc Samuels before she left Mercy to iron out Tina's medical problems and get to the bottom of the latex allergy.

Kate glanced at the photograph of Olivia.

"Jason, didn't you mention a friend of yours who planned to contact World Watch?"

"That's right. Dr. Stan Elders phoned me about a transplant tourist scheme he'd uncovered."

"But it's not a crime for U.S. citizens to have surgeries in foreign countries."

"Medical procedures done in accredited hospitals aren't the issue, Kate. Unethical practices are."

"Meaning the sale of donor organs?"

"Exactly."

"What about follow-up care?"

"That's the problem when patients return to the States. Especially when unscrupulous U.S. physicians get a cut in the package deal. Easy to see why they're less than forthcoming about the risks involved."

"Is that what Dr. Elders suspected?"

"I made notes when he called. Give me a minute to find them."

Kate drummed her fingers on the counter. The articles she'd read on the Internet had detailed the quick-fix mentality that attracted patients desperate for an organ transplant. Less-than-ethical physicians played on their need and sweetened the deal with promises of sightseeing opportunities prior to surgery. Cut-rate prices, organized tours and no mention of how the organs were procured or the likelihood that complications would ensue.

"Here it is," Jason said, coming back on the line. "Stan treated a man who admitted having a transplant in India. The patient was recuperating at a vacation home in Big Bear not far from Stan's office. Seems he developed serious complications. Bottom line, he didn't survive."

"Which can happen even when transplants are done in the States, Jason."

"Unfortunately, yes. But this patient had undergone a thorough post-op workup at the facility that arranged his trip. Stan questioned the clean bill of health they'd given the man just days before Stan treated him. Basic lab tests that would have confirmed the complications were evidently ignored. Stan believed some of the medical records had been falsified."

"But why?"

"Greed, Kate. Word of mouth is how they attract their customers. A patient with complications would hurt business and lower profits."

"That's despicable."

"Absolutely. Unfortunately, Stan was never able to make his suspicions known. I called the authorities after he died, but I didn't have enough details for them to move forward with an investigation."

"Dr. Elders died?"

"Don't you remember that drive-by shooting in Los Angeles involving a research physician?"

"That was Stan Elders?" Kate had caught only a portion of the story on the late-night news. "Wasn't he on his way to a medical conference?"

"That's right. The police claimed it was gang related. Such a shame." Jason let out a deep breath. "Listen, Kate, I hate to cut this short, but Marge just stuck her head in the door. The board of directors is taking a fifteen-minute break. I want talk to them and see how the deliberation's going."

Kate hung up unsettled by what she'd learned. Transplant tourists, falsified records and a drive-by shooting. Olivia had traveled to India and died shortly after her return. Was she involved with the same group of physicians Dr. Elders had suspected?

What Jason had told Kate about Doc Samuels bothered her, as well. More than ever, she wanted to have a chat with the doctor. Find out exactly how he had determined Tina was allergic to latex.

Atlanta traffic snarled through the city bumper to bumper, causing Nolan to keep one foot on the brake pedal and a wary eye on the other lanes of traffic. Fog as thick as smoke hung over the skyline.

"The low visibility is due to a warm front moving in from the Gulf, colliding with colder air from the north," the weatherman announced over the radio. "Expect heavy rains, hail and wind gusts up to forty miles per hour throughout the day."

Exiting Interstate 85 South, Nolan took the off-ramp to the airport, parked in the short-term lot and headed for the terminal.

The concourse teemed with annoyed travelers. One look at the departure board and Nolan knew the reason for their unrest. All planes were delayed for takeoff due to inclement weather. Inbound flights were circling the sky, waiting to land.

Second day in a row when nothing seemed to be going right. Nolan rubbed the back of his neck, hoping to ease the tension that had built up as he approached the nearest red coat.

"Where can I find information about an incoming flight from California?"

The airline agent directed Nolan to the end of a long line of disgruntled customers that slowly snaked toward the information kiosk. Twenty minutes later, Nolan came face-to-face with a tired clerk who shook his head when Nolan inquired about the nonstop flight.

"The plane took off an hour behind schedule. No telling when it will be able to land."

Not the answer Nolan wanted to hear. He stepped away from the counter and made his way to the atrium. Pulling out his cell, he hit the home listing.

Kate answered.

"It's Nolan. Has Tracy Farrington arrived yet?"

"About twenty minutes ago. She's resting at the moment."

Kate's voice sounded cool. Too cool.

Nolan hated that he'd left the house in such a huff. Stupid of him to allow their discussion last night to affect their relationship this morning.

Seeing her in the kitchen had awakened something in him.

She looked so . . . Well, so lovable.

"I won't be back in Mercy until late this afternoon or early evening, but I wanted to ensure Tracy was set to move in. And to thank you for helping me with Heather these last few days."

"I'm afraid I've been a bit of a burden."

"Not at all."

"Nolan, I'd love to have Heather visit me in Atlanta. If that's all right with you."

Kate hadn't mentioned wanting to see Nolan again. "Heather stays pretty busy with school."

"Of course. Probably a bad idea."

"It's just that, well . . ." He wasn't sure why the offer didn't sit well. "Maybe I could drop her off when I have business in the city."

"Certainly. Call me anytime you're in town."

Was that an olive branch? Hard to decipher nuances over the phone.

"Tell Tracy I'll phone her later today. And, Kate? Thanks, again."

Nolan shoved his cell back in his pocket, frustrated. Would he and Kate ever reconnect? A long-distance relationship wasn't his thing. But a few days ago, he hadn't thought any type of a relationship was in his future.

What had changed his mind?

Blue eyes and a feisty woman who didn't understand about God's love.

Hard for people to accept the Lord's love if they had never experienced human love.

Could someone or something change Kate's heart?

The ordeal was almost over. Once Nolan had the evidence he needed, he'd call Kate.

But would she be interested in exploring a relationship or would his window of opportunity have closed by then?

Kate heard Tracy scurry out of the bedroom. Poor dear was probably on her way to the bathroom again.

Tracy pushed open the kitchen door, her face drawn. She carried a towel in her hands. "Can you drive me to the hospital?"

"Is there a problem?"

"Not exactly. It's just that my sister's working a job over in Summerton. I left a message on her cell phone, but I don't know when she'll check her voice mail. Hank's halfway to Caldwell by now and —" Tracy glanced down at the towel. "My water just broke."

"Oh, my gosh. Of course I'll drive you." Without a second's hesitation, Kate wrapped the navy coat around the pregnant woman's shoulders.

Slipping into her own wrap, Kate grabbed a crutch and reached for Tracy's tote. "The car's parked in the garage. Can you make it?"

Tracy nodded and, purse in hand, followed Kate to the garage where she dropped into the front passenger seat of Tina's car. Wedged in place, Tracy looked like a too-ripe melon ready to burst.

"I hate to leave Nolan out on a limb," the pregnant woman sighed.

"Don't give that a thought," Kate assured her.

"Maybe we should leave a note to let him know what happened?"

Kate shook her head. "There's no need. Heather won't be home from school until three-fifteen. I'll be back at the house by then. I can explain everything to Nolan when he returns from his trip."

Rounding the car, Kate tucked her crutch in the back before she slipped into the driver's seat. She grabbed the Velcro straps on the immobilizer, lifted her left leg into the car and scooted the seat back as far as possible.

Kate adjusted her body to take weight off her left hip. Not the most comfortable position, but she had to feel better than Tracy did at the moment.

Turning, Kate stared into her passenger's drawn face. She saw a woman preparing to birth a baby without the support of the man who had played an important role in the situation.

"Want to call the baby's father before we leave?"

A spark of hope flashed across Tracy's face. Evidently, she cared deeply for the man. Then, she shook her head. "He's got a lot of issues to work through right now. I doubt he'd be able to accept a baby into his life. He's so mixed up he doesn't even have time for God."

Kate thought of her own skewed relationship with the Lord. "Maybe you should give him a second chance."

Tracy shook her head again, then grimaced.

Seemed the baby was ready to be born whether the dad was present or not.

"Are you okay?" Kate asked.

Tracy pulled in a deep breath and smiled. "Just ready to get to the hospital. What are we waiting for?"

Kate looked down at the key she clutched in her hand and laughed nervously. "You'll have to direct me."

"Head toward town, then take a right onto the Summerton Road." Another contraction redirected Tracy's attention.

"Fast as those contractions are coming, the MedClinic might be a better option."

Tracy shook her head. "Nolan insisted I deliver at Mountain General in Summerton."

Kate turned the key in the ignition and pressed down on the accelerator.

No time to argue. Kate needed to get Tracy to the hospital. Otherwise, she'd be wishing her chemistry degree had included classes in midwifery.

Sixteen

Kate gripped the wheel with both hands as she steered the small car along the road that steadily climbed to the crest of the Summerton Pass.

The steep descent on the other side unnerved her. Nolan had warned Kate about the spare. Just so the tire wouldn't blow.

Tracy rummaged in her purse and pulled out an envelope. "I forgot. Hank wanted me to give these to Nolan. Would you —"

A contraction hit midsentence. Tracy dropped the envelope to the floor. "Ohhh!" she moaned.

Kate's heart pounded in her chest. "What's wrong?"

The redhead clenched her teeth. "I'm not sure. I've got more pressure. Feels like I need to push."

"No!" Kate knew that much about childbirth. "Whatever you do, don't push. Try to pant instead."

Tracy cried out as the contraction intensified, and for the first time, Kate saw fear in the woman's eyes.

"Pant, Tracy. You can do it."

"I'm . . . I'm scared."

So am I, Kate wanted to add. "We're almost at the hospital." At least she hoped they were.

"Will you pray for me, Kate? Pray for the baby."

"I can't." Kate focused on the road and held the steering wheel even more tightly. "God doesn't listen to my prayers."

"Pl-please," Tracy pleaded, her face contorted as she started to push.

Kate had tried so many times to reach the Almighty, but her prayers — even her pleas for help — had turned on seemingly deaf ears. Why would today be any different?

Because a tiny baby's life hangs in the balance.

The thought flew through her mind. Kate pulled in a strengthening breath. If only she could find the right words.

"God . . . ?"

Would He hear her? Kate glanced at Tracy's face twisted with pain. He *had* to hear her.

"Tracy and her baby need help, Lord. Get . . . Get us to the hospital before this baby comes into the world. And most of all, keep both of them safe."

Almost instantly, Tracy's shoulders relaxed, as if Kate's words had released the tight grip of fear. Tracy pulled in a shallow breath, then blew it out before drawing another and another. Soon, she settled into a steady rhythm as she rubbed her stomach and focused her eyes on the dashboard.

Kate patted Tracy's shoulder reassuringly. "That's great. Keep that rhythm. We're almost there."

Mountain General appeared in the distance. Kate drove to the emergency-room entrance and blared the horn. Two nurses rushed outside.

Opening the passenger door, they quickly assessed the situation. "Looks like we've got a lady ready to deliver."

A sense of relief flowed through Kate. "Thank you, Lord, for getting us here in time."

Pauline arrived fifteen minutes later. Entering the hospital waiting area, she gave Kate a quick hug of thanks.

"God bless you," Pauline said before she hastened to join Tracy in labor and delivery.

Kate looked at her watch as she left Mountain General. Before Heather arrived home from school, Kate wanted to stop by

Dr. Samuels's office to pick up the final medical report on her leg injury, as well as clear up this latex mystery once and for all.

If Nolan got home early enough, Kate would have the tire changed and drive back to Atlanta as she had planned. Worst-case scenario, she could stay overnight and leave in the morning.

As Kate hobbled toward the parking lot, she nearly bumped into a man walking determinedly toward the hospital entrance.

Jimmy Ramos's brother. "Miguel?"

Hearing his name, he stopped, brow raised. "Kate. Sorry, I didn't see you."

"Everything okay? I hope Jimmy's not sick."

He shook his head. "No, it's . . ." Miguel hesitated. "A friend of mine's having a baby."

"Tracy Farrington?"

Surprise washed over his face. "How'd you know?"

"I drove her to the hospital. She's in labor and delivery on the second floor. Her sister arrived about five minutes ago."

"Pauline called me on her way over here. Luckily, I was in Summerton on business."

"So you and Tracy —"

"Ah . . ." He chewed on his lip and shrugged. "It's complicated."

An unwed mother and a baby on the way. Oh, yeah, looked like things were really complicated.

Kate pointed to the hospital. "Don't let me keep you."

He nodded before hurrying toward the entrance.

Finding Tina's car, Kate slid into the driver's seat and stuck the key in the ignition.

The envelope Tracy had left for Nolan lay open on the floor of the passenger's side. Kate reached to pick it up.

A photo fell out.

Kate gasped.

The photo showed Dr. Samuels standing over a dead body. The person on the stretcher was her dear friend Tina Espinosa.

Seventeen

"He's at Agnes Heartwell's house," Dr. Samuels's secretary informed Kate when she stopped by his office. "Take this form. You need the doctor to sign the request before I can release your medical records."

Frustrated with the red tape involved in gaining a copy of her own records, Kate drove to Ms. Agnes's house and rang the doorbell.

The brick ranch sat high atop Mercy Mountain with the valley visible below. The tops of the tall pine trees and a view of Mercy High stretched in the distance.

Kate pushed the bell twice and shouted through the door. "Ms. Agnes, it's Kate Murphy. We met at Tina's funeral. I'm looking for Dr. Samuels."

The door inched open. Instead of Agnes, Edith Turner's square face stared back at Kate. The nurse placed her large hand on the edge of the door frame. "What?"

Kate drew in a fortifying breath. "I need to talk to Dr. Samuels."

Edith glanced outside and opened the door far enough for Kate and her crutch to sidle through. "Aggie's in the living room with Sue Ann."

Kate headed in the direction Edith pointed and entered the large living area. The far wall was rimmed with picture windows that showcased the breathtaking view of the backside of the mountain. A narrow dirt road wound around the house and disappeared down a steep rear incline.

Agnes lounged on a large overstuffed couch and stood as Kate walked into the room. "Why, dear, what a nice surprise."

Sue Ann sat in a wheelchair near the fireplace. Her hands were folded on her lap, and a colorful afghan covered her legs. Brown hair hung thick around her pale face. Sue Ann's eyes were closed, and her mouth sagged open.

As Kate stepped closer, she blinked her eyes open. Sue Ann's pupils appeared dilated, her tongue thick as she tried to speak. "H-h-h-help . . . Help me, please."

Agnes moved to her daughter's side and rubbed her hand over Sue Ann's arm. "There, there, sugar. Don't you fret. Edith's gonna make you right comfortable."

Agnes nodded to Edith, who stepped to the rear of the wheelchair and rolled Sue Ann from the room.

The disabled woman reached out for Kate as she passed. "P-p-please help me!"

A tear ran down Agnes's cheek. She wiped it away with a swipe of her hand and sniffed. "Sue Ann's condition has gotten worse since Sunday. That upper respiratory infection's taking a toll."

Sue Ann seemed to be struggling with something more than a URI. The woman's eyes held the same empty look Kate had seen in Eddie's eyes that night at the cabin.

An infection was a concern, but Sue Ann appeared to have another problem. Over-medication.

Kate held up the medical-record release form. "I need Dr. Samuels to sign this, Ms. Agnes. His secretary said I'd find him here."

"And you would have. But he got a call that Tracy Farrington was having labor pains."

"So he's at the hospital in Summerton?"

"No, dear. He said he was headed to Tracy's house. She lives with her sister Pauline."

"But —"

"Sit down, Kate. I'll ask Edith to make us some tea. Then I'll call Lloyd and tell him you want to see him. I'm sure he can swing by later."

"But I saw Pauline in Summerton."

"She cleans houses, don't you know. Probably had a job there this morning. She's home now."

Pauline couldn't be home. Kate had left her not more than forty-five minutes ago at the hospital.

Had someone given Ms. Agnes the wrong information about Samuels? "Pauline wouldn't have asked Doc Samuels to stop by her house, Ms. Agnes. Tracy's ready to deliver her baby at the hospital."

A perplexed look spread over the old woman's face. "Maybe I got confused."

"I'm sure it was a mix-up of some sort," Kate reassured her.

"Why yes, dear. Sometimes I'm so forgetful. Tina even mentioned it. My, but Sue Ann looked forward to Tina's visits."

Kate thought of what Tina had written in her journal. "Did Tina tell you she was worried about your daughter?"

"What do you mean, dear?"

"Tina felt Sue Ann had become depressed and paranoid. Could it have been the medication Dr. Samuels prescribed?"

Before Kate could say more, Edith stepped back into living room, carrying a tray with two cups of tea.

"Why, Edith, how thoughtful of you." Agnes motioned for Kate to join her on the couch. "I'm sure you'll enjoy Edith's special brew."

Placing the tray on the coffee table, the nurse gave Agnes one of the cups and offered the other to Kate, who shook her head. "I really can't stay."

"But, dear, what about the form Lloyd needs to sign?" Agnes asked.

Kate glanced from Agnes's questioning eyes to Edith, who still held the cup of hot tea. "I'll stop by his office later."

Agnes raised her brow and looked at Edith. "Kate says someone gave me the wrong information about Lloyd. Evidently, Tracy's ready to deliver at the hospital."

Edith turned cold eyes toward Kate.

"Please —" Sue Ann's voice echoed from the rear of the house. "Help me!"

Agnes waved at Edith. "You see to Sue Ann."

The nurse placed the cup on the table before she scurried from the room.

Agnes pointed to the tea. "Why don't you take a few sips before you leave?"

"I can't stay. Nolan's out of town, and Heather's due home from school in a few minutes. I'll call you later. We can talk about Sue Ann then."

"Thank you for stopping by, dear. You know your way out, don't you?"

"Of course." Crutch in hand, Kate limped to the door, relieved to have escaped before Edith came back into the living room.

A shiver slipped down Kate's spine. She'd be glad once she got back to the security of Nolan's house. Right now, she felt about as vulnerable as a rabbit in a trap.

A weather update flashed on an overhead monitor in the airport atrium. All around Nolan, disgruntled travelers strained to listen to the latest forecast.

"Torrential rains continue to pound the southeast. High winds have caused major power outages, and a second band of storm cells threatens to wreak additional damage throughout the night as it heads north through Georgia."

Weather couldn't get much worse. Nolan shook his head. Not the night he wanted to be away from Heather.

His phone vibrated. Nolan flipped it open and heard Dave's strained voice.

"Another problem on this end," the P.I. said.

"Yeah?"

"Sanjeer Hira. Seems he left his office for a meeting and never returned. They found

238

the doctor at his Beverly Hills mansion. Dead. Brains blown out with a nine millimeter."

"Suicide?"

"More like murder. The homicide guys are staking out their turf. Not the friendliest group. At this point, no one's focused on the transplant tourist scheme."

Nolan needed everything tied up nice and neat. But with Hira's murder, the situation was growing far more sinister than he had ever imagined.

His first priority was to make sure Heather was safe. The way things were progressing, he wanted his daughter far away from Mercy and anything involved with the transplant tourist scheme. "I'll call you later, Dave."

Nolan disconnected, then hit the home listing. "Heather, how's the weather?"

"Dad?" Her voice wavered.

A group of tourists standing behind Nolan started to chatter loudly. He threw them an irritated look, decided they weren't about to quiet and headed to an empty corner by a bank of wall phones.

"Now I can hear you, hon. What's wrong?"

"I just got home from school, and no one's here. I thought Tracy was coming over to stay for a few days?"

A nervous tingle pricked Nolan's neck. "Maybe she's outside?"

"No. I even checked Tina's apartment. The strange thing is that Tina's car's not here, either."

Nolan let out a deep breath. "Kate had to go back to Atlanta. She took the Honda."

"But that's just it, Dad. Kate's clothes are neatly packed in a plastic bag sitting in the hallway."

A sense of dread spread over Nolan. "I'm coming home. Lock the doors. Don't let anyone in."

He glanced out the terminal windows. Rain plummeted to the earth. "A storm's heading north. Keep the radio on for updates. Do your homework in my office if things get too bad." He paused. "And, Heather . . ."

"Yeah, Dad."

"I love you, honey."

Kate climbed into the car she had parked outside Agnes Heartwell's home and slanted a quick glance down the narrow dirt road that led from the front of the house to the valley below. The sheriff's squad car zoomed up the hill, a cloud of dust billowing out in its wake.

Not wanting anything to do with Edith or

her sheriff husband, Kate steered the car
around the house and headed down the rear
path she'd noticed earlier.

Trees and underbrush cleared momentarily, providing a view of the highway Kate
and Heather had driven along yesterday.
Also visible was the trail at the edge of the
Hawkins farm where Tina's body had been
found.

In the distance, the roof of the log cabin
Heather had mentioned peeked through the
foliage. Kate's eyes caught sight of something else, not far from the cabin.

An aluminum building.

At that instant, another clump of vegetation obstructed her view.

The road dipped. Kate lifted her foot from
the gas pedal and pushed down on the
brake.

The car failed to decelerate. She glanced
at the speedometer. Thirty-five miles per
hour.

Kate pumped the pedal.

A downward slope stretched ahead. The
car gained speed. Forty miles per hour,
fifty . . .

Kate tried to lift her left leg to the emergency brake. The immobilizer prevented any
movement.

Her heart pounded. Fear roared in her

ears along with the rush of wind.

She shifted in her seat and edged her right leg over the injured one.

Sixty miles per hour.

Her right foot connected with the emergency pedal. She pushed down. The brake failed to hold.

A curve —

Kate turned the wheel. The car skidded.

A cluster of trees loomed ahead. Kate screamed as the car crashed into the tall pines.

With a whoosh, the airbag exploded against her chest.

Knocked out for a second, Kate's head swam as she opened her eyes.

Get out of the car.

She tried to pull free, but the airbag pinned her against the seat.

She groped for the door handle.

"Kate, you okay?" Sheriff Turner stood next to the car.

"Help me," she mumbled.

He pried the door open. "Everything's gonna be okay." Grabbing her shoulders, he pulled her from the car.

The world swirled around her. Kate saw movement out of the corner of her eye. She turned.

Edith Turner stood just a few steps away,

a sadistic smirk spread over her square jaw. She grabbed Kate's arm.

"You're hurting me." Kate tried to jerk free.

Edith strengthened her hold and laughed. The sound made Kate's skin crawl. Her heart thumped wildly, and fear gripped her anew.

In a moment of desperation, Kate raked the nails of her free hand over the nurse's arm.

Edith screamed as four red welts instantly appeared. Rearing back, she raised her hand and slammed her fist into Kate's jaw.

Suddenly, the world collapsed from under Kate, and everything went black.

EIGHTEEN

The rain eased momentarily as Nolan left the airport terminal and raced for short-term parking. Once in his SUV, he removed his cell from his pocket, called information and tapped in the first of two numbers he had requested.

The answering machine clicked on at Kate's home. He disconnected and tried her Atlanta lab.

A woman answered on the third ring. "Jason Bannister's office. How may I help you?"

"My name's Nolan Price. Kate Murphy and I are friends."

Would he ever have the chance to be more?

"I was wondering if someone at your lab might know her current whereabouts."

"Jason Bannister spoke to Kate earlier. He's still in his office. I'll put you through."

Kate's boss. Might as well start at the top.

When Jason came on the line, Nolan gave him a short version of why he needed to locate Kate. "She didn't answer her home phone, and I thought she may have stopped by work on her way into Atlanta."

"Last I heard she was attending a friend's funeral in northern Georgia."

"Mercy. That's right. She was staying at my place. My daughter and I —"

"Kate mentioned you. Listen, I wouldn't worry. She probably stopped to grab a bite to eat. If she calls, I'll let her know you're looking for her, Mr. Price. And if you talk to her first, well . . ." Jason hesitated. "I'd like to be the one to tell her, but I know she's eager to hear. No reason to sit on good news. Tell Kate the board decided in her favor. Not that the Atlanta papers did us any favors. I'm sure Kate told you what happened."

"She said something about a news article."

"You should be proud of her," Jason said. "I have to admit, at first I was in favor of the Southern Technology merger. Thought it would be a good thing for Bannister Scientific. But Kate stood her ground. She'd seen how South Tech cut corners. That's not the way Bannister wants to operate. After a review of her documentation, we pulled out of the deal. Tell Kate I've submitted a letter to the editor that should appear in tomorrow's newspaper. Gives Kate the recognition she deserves."

She had stood firm against the pressure to change and had won. A warmth spread over Nolan. He *was* proud of Kate.

More than anything, he wanted to reconnect with her. Was she on her way back to Atlanta? Or was she still in Mercy? If so, where?

"Did Kate mention anything else, Jason, that might explain where she is?"

"Just that she wanted to talk to the town physician."

"Lloyd Samuels?"

"Of course you'd know him. Kate said Samuels is the only doctor in town. Funny, last I heard he was working with a Beverly Hills researcher."

Nolan gripped the phone more tightly. A tingle of anticipation rolled through his gut.

"Who'd he work with, Jason? I used to live in L.A. Might be someone I know."

"I couldn't remember when I was talking to Kate, but the name came to me not long ago. Met the guy at a medical conference in San Francisco. Ever hear of Sanjeer Hira?"

Nolan's heart thumped against his rib cage.

"Yeah. I have heard of him." Nolan asked

Jason to call him if he talked to Kate. Then, he closed his phone and turned the key in his ignition. He needed to get back to Mercy. Nothing was as crucial as making sure Heather and Kate were safe.

A sharp pain sliced across Kate's jaw. She tried to move but couldn't.

Her head ached. Saliva pooled in the back of her throat. She gagged against the thick wad of cloth jammed in her mouth.

"Glad to see you're coming around."

Kate's eyes opened. Lloyd Samuels stood over her.

"Don't worry, my dear. You're safe with me." His fingers touched the edge of the stretcher upon which she lay. Two restraining straps held her down.

Unable to get her bearings, Kate glanced around the room. Not the MedClinic she remembered.

Tile covered the walls and floor. A stainless steel cabinet filled with medical supplies stood against the far wall.

Where was she?

Lloyd chuckled. "This is a private facility reserved for my out-of-town guests. They appreciate the anonymity I provide them. Lack of accreditation and governmental regulations has its advantages."

247

Kate's vision blurred and a wave of nausea overpowered her. She blinked, willing the room back into focus.

He patted her arm. "Now, now, Kate. Of course you're disoriented. You were in an accident. Remember?"

She tried to think. She had left Agnes Heartwell's house, heading down the hill when —

"You probably want me to tell Nolan you're hurt, now don't you, Kate?"

She glared up at him and wiggled her fingers and toes, grateful they responded to her prompting.

"It's not as bad as it seems. Thanks to your airbag deploying, you suffered no bodily harm, although I know you've been shaken up."

His smile sent a chill down her spine. She struggled to free herself from the restraints but to no avail.

Lloyd laughed. "Don't worry. I'm not going to kill you. At least not yet. I'll keep you alive for a few more days."

Her stomach roiled. She turned her head to the side as another wave of nausea swept over her.

"There, there. Why don't you rest? I'll be back later."

As soon as Lloyd closed the door behind

him, Kate screamed into the gag, but a muffled moan was the only sound she heard.

Leaving the gridlock of Atlanta traffic behind, Nolan reached for his cell and called Dave. "Airport's still shut down due to weather. No arrivals or departures and no chance to connect with Mrs. Preston. But I did learn the name of Sanjeer Hira's former research partner."

"Things are falling into place," Dave said when Nolan filled him in on the details. "There's a lot of speculation about the clinical director's death. LAPD hauled in a suspect for questioning. His wife had recently died from a massive infection. Guess who her doctor was?"

"Sanjeer Hira."

"You got that right. My guess, they'll discover the man's wife had undergone a transplant outside the United States and died of complications."

"You think hubby decided to take the law into his own hands?"

"Looks that way."

"I'm beginning to think I got involved in something far bigger than I ever imagined."

"Just take care of yourself and your daughter. What about that woman who was Tina's friend?"

Nolan shook his head. "I don't know where she is, Dave, and I'm concerned."

"I hear it in your voice."

Raindrops splattered against the windshield. "The weather's getting worse, and you're starting to break up. Keep me posted, Dave."

"Good luck, buddy."

Nolan clicked off and threw the phone onto the passenger seat. He'd need more than luck.

Lord, let me find Kate.

Over the last few days, Kate had become more than just Tina's friend. She'd taken up residence in Nolan's heart, as well as his home.

But where was she?

Heather was worried. So was Nolan.

Kate heard two people talking, their voices muffled.

Her head pounded. She longed for a cool cloth and a comforting word.

The voices offered neither.

"You've gone too far this time, Lloyd," a woman warned.

"Now don't scold me, Janelle." He laughed.

"Oh, Lloyd. You're crazy."

"Crazy in love with you."

"Shush," she teased. "You know I'm a married woman."

"You *should* be married to me. Divorce Wade."

"In due time."

"I don't want to wait."

"When your research is done. When you've proved regeneration works." She laughed again. "Then I'll marry you, Lloyd."

Footsteps. A door closed. Silence.

Kate opened her eyes. Regeneration?

The house was ablaze with light as Nolan pulled into the driveway, grabbed his keys from the ignition and raced inside. "Heather?"

Where was she? "Honey?"

He opened the door to the basement.

"I'm in your office, Dad."

Relief flooded him as he scurried down the stairs and met his daughter halfway. Her face was pale and drawn with worry.

"Have you talked to Kate?" he asked, hearing the concern in his own voice.

"No. I phoned Tracy's house. No one's there, either. What's going on?"

"I don't know, honey."

"Don't know or won't tell me?"

The challenge Nolan saw in his daughter's eyes made him realize Kate was right.

Heather was a young woman who needed to hear the truth.

"Dad, you didn't tell me everything about Mom's condition and look what happened. Even though I'm young, I could tell things had changed between you two. Mom had her work, and you . . ." She stared at him for a long second.

Nolan wondered what his daughter saw. A man who struggled to do what was right or the authoritative parent he'd become?

"You didn't realize I was growing up, Dad."

His throat thickened. "Oh, Heather, I'm so sorry. I should have listened when you asked me not to go on that trip after Mom returned from India."

He explained about the real-estate agent's call. The perfect home for the three of them in San Francisco wouldn't stay on the market long. A new home would mean a chance for a new start.

Heather sighed. "Mom never confided in me. That's why I was scared when you left. I knew she wouldn't tell me how she really felt. She was doing okay. Then she got worse in the night. The next morning —"

Tears filled Heather's eyes. "She didn't want me to call the doctor. She said she wouldn't go to the hospital."

Nolan wrapped his arms around his grieving daughter and kissed her forehead.

She pushed back and looked into his eyes. "I tried to blame you for Mom's death. But down deep, I really blamed myself."

Nolan's heart tore in two. "You didn't do anything wrong, Heather. You loved your mother, and you were following her wishes, being the good daughter you've always been."

He rubbed his hand over her back as she buried her head in his chest and sobbed, the pain and guilt she'd carried all these months finally exposed.

He held her close as tears streamed down her face. When she started to calm, he reached into his back pocket and pulled out his handkerchief.

She wiped the cloth over her cheeks and sniffed.

"There's something else I have to tell you." Her eyes filled once again. "What happened to Tina was my fault."

"Honey, you're eaten with guilt. I'm the one who insisted we move to Mercy."

"But Tina and I both liked it here," Heather quickly interjected. "Once she got to know the people at church, she said she found new meaning to her life. She loved being able to help others. Sue Ann was important to her. She and Tracy were friends, and Tina planned to help with the baby."

"You gave Tina nothing but joy, Heather."

She shook her head and pulled out of his embrace. "Last Thursday night when you were gone, I snuck out of the house."

His head reeled. "What?"

"I don't blame you for being mad, Dad. But I have to tell you everything."

A heavy weight settled on Nolan's shoulders. His neck tightened, and he consciously willed his muscles to relax. He trusted his daughter. He hoped he could trust his reactions when she told him what had happened.

Pulling in a steadying breath, he said, "Honey, I love you, and I do trust you."

He prayed his words rang true to Heather's ears. What would Kate tell him to do? She had given him good advice when it came to his daughter. "You can tell me anything, honey. I'm here to help."

"Jimmy was worried about a friend of his who had gotten a bad grade on an algebra exam. The boy's brother was one of those kids involved in that crash on the mountain road a few weeks ago. He was upset and told Jimmy life wasn't worth living. Some of the kids hang out at that old cabin on Mr.

Hawkins's farm."

She hesitated.

"Go on, Heather," he encouraged.

"Jimmy didn't want me to get in trouble, but I was worried about him going out there alone. So I snuck out and met him along the main road."

The idea of Heather alone in the night, waiting for Jimmy Ramos to pick her up, chilled Nolan to the core.

"You were away on business, and Tina must have heard me. She followed us to the cabin. Jimmy's friend was there. He was crying 'cause he missed his brother. I know God led Jimmy there to comfort his friend." She looked at Nolan with adult eyes. "He had a bottle of prescription pills and said he would have taken his life if we hadn't arrived when we did."

A tight feeling gripped Nolan's chest. "What happened then?"

"Tina showed up. She told Jimmy to take his friend home to his parents. She gave me a good lecture. Said I'd made a big mistake going there. That it was dangerous."

Nolan's skin crawled. "Dangerous in what way?"

"She saw something in the woods but wouldn't tell me what. Tina had planned to go back the next day. That's where they found her car. On the dirt road, not far from the cabin. If I hadn't gone out there Thursday night, Tina wouldn't have returned the next day. Then she wouldn't have had the flat tire and tried to change it." Heather's face clouded again. "Don't you see it's all my fault?"

Nolan placed his hands on Heather's shoulders. "No, honey. You had nothing to do with Tina's death."

"I'm so sorry I snuck out, Dad."

"And I'm sorry for being headstrong and stubborn and for not being there when you needed me."

She gave him a quick hug, then pulled back. "I'm worried about Kate. You've got to look for her."

"I can't leave you alone in this storm."

"Of course you can," she said determinedly. "I'll be all right."

Nolan thought of the cabin and the pictures Pauline had seen. Had Kate gotten tangled up with Lloyd?

"I want to talk to Dr. Samuels, then I'll check the cabin and see what I can find." Nolan dropped a kiss on Heather's upturned cheek. "I love you, honey."

"I love you, too, Dad."

Nolan raced through the rain to his car. A huge burden had lifted from his shoulders.

He and Heather had bridged the gap in their relationship. But an even heavier sense of dread filtered over him.

He knew with certainty Kate was in grave danger.

Nineteen

Kate rolled her head to the side, fighting another wave of nausea, willing herself not to be sick. Not here. Not with a gag in her mouth.

Her head throbbed. If her upset stomach didn't get her, the headache would. She twisted her torso and pushed against the restraints. Pain sailed up her thigh.

She was fighting for her life. A hurt leg was the least of her worries.

Closing her eyes, she waited until her stomach calmed.

If only her mind would focus so she could think her way out of this mess.

Listening for any sound that might warn of Janelle and Lloyd's return, Kate heard nothing except her pounding heart and labored breathing.

Again, she pushed against the restraints. They held fast. Wiggling her fingers, she tried to pull her hand free. She strained with the effort and felt a surge of hope when her hand moved ever so slightly.

She tried again. And again.

The thick, abrasive strap scraped against her flesh, rubbing her skin raw. Her hand stung like fire, but she wouldn't give up.

Another inch or two and she'd be free.

Footsteps sounded in the hallway just before the door pushed open. Lloyd stepped toward the stretcher and leered down at her.

Lord, don't let him notice my hand.

"I hope you rested, my dear?"

Kate refused to make a sound.

Lloyd tilted his head as he reached for the gag. "Why don't I remove this so we can chat?"

He ripped the tape off her cheek and yanked the cloth from her mouth.

She cried out.

"Did I hurt you?"

"Why are you holding me captive?" she demanded as soon as she found her voice.

"Now, Kate, that's not the tone I want to hear."

The man was crazy, no doubt about it. She needed to keep her wits about her and proceed with caution.

Lowering her voice, Kate tried to sound sincere. "Please, Lloyd, let me go. I won't tell anyone about your secret clinic."

"Do you know what I'm working on?"

"My guess, organ regeneration."

"Smart as a whip, aren't you? But you're right. A scientific breakthrough in liver regeneration, and it's all mine."

He chuckled. "I won't bore you with all the details. Suffice it to say that my success rate is astounding. Patients will no longer be forced to travel to foreign countries to procure an organ."

"You're involved in a transplant tourist scheme, aren't you, Lloyd? Only your patients never hear about the dangers. You're part of the operation Stan Elders found out about."

"Foreign medicine is never as exact as in the United States, Kate. At least my pretransplant treatment increases organ viability. But someone was asking too many questions, so I made sure he was taken care of."

"You killed Dr. Elders?"

"I didn't pull the trigger, Kate. The police decided it was gang warfare."

"What about Tina?"

"She found this clinic. I had to kill her. Along with a few others."

"You're evil."

Lloyd laughed, a diabolical sound that echoed through the room. "No, Kate. I'm a genius and the world will soon recognize me as such. I'm working with a group of physicians who understand the importance of regenerative medicine. They'll help me market my organs around the world."

"Committed physicians don't deal in underhanded schemes."

"You think you're so high and mighty, don't you, Kate? I'll show you who's got the upper hand now."

He grabbed her chin.

"No!" she screamed before he jammed the gag back into her mouth.

Dr. Samuels rolled a steel cart with surgical instruments over to the stretcher.

Kate glanced at the cart. Her eyes focused on the razor-sharp scalpel.

If she could only pull her hand free.

Nolan left Heather and drove through the pouring rain to Lloyd's office. The receptionist said he'd left earlier in the day to check on Sue Ann.

Climbing back into his SUV, Nolan called Ms. Aggie on his cell.

"Lloyd was here this afternoon," she said. "He didn't tell me where he was headed."

"Would you phone me, Aggie, if he stops by again?"

"Sure I will, Nolan. You and Heather have

a good night."

Nolan canvassed the town before driving to the cabin. Stepping inside, he was surprised to find the interior clean and neat. Four overstuffed chairs and a couch that had seen better days sat in front of a large stone fireplace. Textbooks filled a small bookcase in the corner.

Heather said the kids sometimes met there to study. Nolan breathed a sigh of relief. His daughter had told him the truth.

Back outside, he shielded his eyes from the driving rain and scanned the surrounding woods. Tina had seen something when she'd followed Heather to the cabin. But what?

The area was densely forested with pines and hardwoods. Anything could be hidden in the thick vegetation.

Rain pounded the windshield as Nolan turned his SUV back onto the dirt road where Tina's body had been found. He flipped the wipers to high and slowly drove along the narrow lane, looking for any sign of Kate.

Thunder rumbled overhead as lightning illuminated the night sky. Nolan dug his cell from his pocket and pushed the home listing.

"Any news from Kate?" he asked when

Heather answered.

"Not a word, Dad. I phoned Tracy's house again, but no one answers there, either."

"The storm's gaining strength. Get a flashlight in case the electricity goes off. I want to check a few more spots before I come home."

"Be careful."

"You too, honey. I wish you weren't alone."

"But I'm not. Ms. Agnes is here."

"What?"

"Edith's taking care of Sue Ann. Ms. Aggie said she can stay with me until either you or Kate return home."

Nolan hadn't mentioned Kate when he'd spoken with Agnes on the phone or that Heather was home alone. "Did you tell Ms. Aggie that Kate was gone?"

"Why no, Dad. We've been talking about school and how we both like science and math."

Static crackled across the line. "What was that?"

". . . science and math . . ."

"Heather?"

Silence.

Nolan pulled the cell from his ear. *Call failed.*

He hit Redial. The screen went blank.

He needed to turn around and head home. A bend in the road lay ahead. The flash of police lights broke through the darkness.

Nolan recognized the sheriff's sedan parked next to a clump of trees where an auto had crashed into the tall pines.

Nolan pulled up to the clearing and stepped from his car. His stomach churned as he approached the wreck.

Tina's Honda.

"Kate," he screamed and ran for the car.

Hands grabbed him. "Whoa, there, buddy. Not so fast."

Nolan pivoted, his hands fisted, ready to fight off the person holding him back.

Sheriff Wayne Turner.

"Let go of me, Turner. I have to find Kate. Where is she? The MedClinic?"

"Another facility. I'll take you there."

Nolan looked at Turner's twisted smile and knew the truth. The sheriff was one of the wolves in sheep's clothing.

Anger welled within Nolan. He wrenched out of the sheriff's hold. "Tell me what you've done with her."

Something rustled behind Nolan. He turned just as a large, heavy object slammed into the side of his head.

■ ■ ■ ■

The lights flickered briefly as Kate worked her hand against the restraint, the rough strap cutting her flesh. Almost free.

Two male voices approached from the hallway.

Kate couldn't make out what they were saying over the clatter of a cart being pushed along the tile floor. She closed her eyes and forced her body to appear relaxed.

The door clicked open.

"He knows too much."

Kate recognized Lloyd's voice. If only he would think she was asleep.

"Hate to tell you, but Wade's been grumbling about wanting out, Doc. Might be a problem, as well."

"I can handle him, Wayne."

Sheriff Turner?

The cart came to a halt next to her stretcher. The smell of cigarette smoke wafted through the air.

"What the —"

Kate opened her eyes a slit. Darkness except for the red glow of a cigarette butt dangling from the sheriff's mouth.

"The storm must be messing with the power lines, Doc."

"Find Edith. Tell her to sedate both of them. I'll fill the generator with gasoline in case the storm knocks the electricity out completely."

Both of them? The lights flicked on. Kate ventured a peek over the edge of the stretcher.

A body lay on the utility cart.

Nolan!

She clenched her teeth to keep from making a sound.

The sheriff and Lloyd left the room, closing the door behind them.

Kate yanked her hand from under the restraint and pulled the gag out of her mouth.

"Nolan?" she whispered, praying he could hear her.

His eyebrows twitched, but his eyes remained closed. A nasty red lump stood out on his forehead, and a deep gash cut across the top of his skull. Blood splattered his jacket and white shirt.

She stretched her hand toward the surgical tray where the scalpel lay on the green cotton cloth. Grabbing the cold steel, she sliced through the two restraints that held her bound.

Rolling off the stretcher, Kate steadied herself. Her knee was painful but would hold her weight, Kate hoped. She bent down to where Nolan lay on the bed of the utility cart just inches off the floor.

"Can you hear me, Nolan?" She rubbed her hands tenderly over his cheeks, taking care not to touch the lump on his forehead.

He groaned.

She tugged at the ropes binding his hands and legs. They refused to loosen. Taking the scalpel, she sliced through the thick hemp.

Kate rubbed his wrists, relieved when she felt a pulse.

He opened his eyes. "Kate," he rasped.

"What happened?"

"Tina's car. Looked . . . like an accident. I . . . I thought you'd been hurt."

"Tina told me she'd seen something in the woods. She must have found this building," Kate whispered.

"And died because of it. Evidently, Lloyd killed anyone who happened to discover this hidden clinic. Wade took photos of the doc with five of his victims."

"I saw. Tracy had pictures she wanted to give you."

Nolan winced. "Is she okay?"

Kate smiled reassuringly. "Safe and sound in labor and delivery. Her baby has probably been born by now."

He let out a sigh of relief. "Thank God."

Footsteps sounded outside the door. Kate repositioned the ropes around Nolan's hands and legs. She crawled back onto the stretcher, stuck the gag in her mouth and laid the restraints over herself as the door opened. Edith Turner walked into the room.

Out of the corner of her eye, Kate watched the nurse remove two syringes from the drawer and two vials from the drug cart. She filled one syringe, tapped the shaft with her forefinger and expelled a few drops of excess fluid.

Kate tensed as Edith approached the stretcher. Unwrapping an alcohol swab, she wiped the cool square across Kate's arm.

Just as the nurse raised the syringe, Nolan grabbed Edith's ankles, throwing her off balance.

She gasped. Fell. Her head hit the tile floor with a loud crack, knocking her unconscious.

The syringe rolled across the floor.

Kate slipped off the stretcher and reached for the hypodermic. Sheathing the needle, she tucked the syringe into her pocket.

Nolan moaned as he stood, using the edge of the stretcher for support. Blood oozed from the wound on his head. Quickly removing the ropes that had held him bound, he used them to tie Edith's hands and feet.

Kate searched through the drawers until she found surgical tape. Jamming a stack of four-by-four gauze squares into Edith's mouth, she taped it shut.

One thing for certain, Edith wasn't going anywhere soon.

"Let me bandage your head," Kate whispered to Nolan. "You're losing so much blood."

"We don't have time." Ashen-faced, Nolan squeezed her hand before he reached for the door. The lights flickered again but didn't go out.

"Dear Lord, protect us," Kate whispered.

Nolan nodded in agreement, then turned the knob. Peering into the great expanse of the building, he saw a row of refrigerator units, a large freezer, centrifuges, a microscope and lab benches. Lloyd had a full-scale operation going.

Nolan had searched the MedClinic and Lloyd's home, never imagining he'd find a state-of-the-art medical facility hidden in the woods.

But Tina had found it first. And it had cost her life.

Nolan looked at Kate. Her delicate profile made him want to reach out and caress her cheek. Instead, he pushed her behind him, shielding her as best he could.

Lord, let nothing happen to her.

Too many people had died. Nolan would do anything — even sacrifice his own life — to save Kate.

The clinic appeared deserted. Nolan eased the door open far enough for both of them to slip through.

A side exit appeared to be their best escape route. He signaled Kate. Cautiously, they advanced.

Ten feet from the exit, a bay door at the front of the clinic rumbled open. A blue sedan drove into the expansive interior.

Wade Green sat behind the wheel, a scowl on his face. Ms. Agnes Heartwell occupied the passenger seat, eyes wide, lips pursed.

Nolan's heart rose to his throat. "Oh, God, no!" he cried.

A third person was wedged between them. "Heather!"

TWENTY

A sickening fear gripped Kate. *Not Heather!*

Agnes stepped from the sedan and pulled Heather out behind her. The girl's face was as white as snow. Her eyes gleamed with fear. She spied her father and blanched even more.

Kate followed the girl's gaze. Blood seeped steadily from Nolan's wound, soaking his shirt. Too much blood.

"Dad?" Heather's voice was racked with fear.

"Come here, honey."

She ran into his outstretched arms. "Oh, Dad, I'm so sorry. Ms. Agnes said you were hurt —"

"It's okay." He rubbed her back reassuringly then gently pushed her into Kate's arms.

Kate drew her close and held her tight.

The side door opened. Lloyd stepped inside. His eyes darted from the newcomers and Nolan to where Kate tried to comfort the trembling teen.

"Now, isn't this a coincidence? Everyone's here." Lloyd wiped his hands on a damp rag and tossed it onto the floor near the door. The smell of gasoline wafted through the air.

Nolan's hands fisted. "Get out of our way, Lloyd."

Lloyd glanced at the funeral director. "Wade, take the girl —"

Nolan turned and glared defiantly at Wade. "Don't touch my daughter." He pointed to the exit. "Kate, you and Heather head for the door."

Kate nudged the girl forward.

What was Agnes doing? The woman had returned to the car and was searching for something in her purse. As she stepped clear of the sedan, the hair on Kate's neck tingled. Ms. Agnes held a gun in her hand.

Kate pulled Heather up short and moved protectively in front of her.

Lloyd laughed nervously. "Now, Aggie, what are you doing? You don't know how to shoot."

The old woman squared her shoulders and aimed the gun at Lloyd. "I know enough to pull the trigger. You lied to me about Sue Ann's surgery. My husband and

I set you up in this clinic because you said you were committed to making our daughter walk."

"And I still am. But spinal cord regeneration is a long stretch from what we're doing now. All I need is a little more time, Aggie."

"And money?" Agnes waved the gun at him. "That's what you wanted all along, isn't it? Someone to fund your research. Too bad those Beverly Hills doctors weren't interested in regeneration."

"But they are now, Aggie. They'll help me market my organs throughout the world. We're close." Lloyd pointed to Kate and Heather and sneered. "Once we get rid of these problems, I'll have time to finish the regeneration project."

"You're scum, Lloyd." Nolan lunged for the doc.

The side door burst open. Wayne Turner stepped inside. Tossing his cigarette butt aside, the sheriff tackled Nolan, who threw a left jab that connected with Turner's jaw.

Lloyd grabbed a beaker and slammed the heavy vessel against Nolan's head.

Glass shattered across the floor.

"Ahhh." Nolan staggered backward, blood spraying from his wound. The sheriff wrenched Nolan's arms behind his back.

"No!" Heather cried.

Kate shoved the girl behind a large steel freezer.

Lloyd nodded toward the funeral director. "Wade, take that gun from Aggie."

Wade snatched the weapon out of Agnes's hand. "Doc knows what's best, Ms. Aggie."

"He's using you, Wade. Just like he used me. You ever ask Janelle about those special treatments Lloyd's been giving her when you're tied up with a funeral?"

"Shut up, Aggie," the doc demanded.

Uncertainty washed over Wade's face. "What treatments?"

Agnes shook her head and tsked. "Don't be a fool, Wade. Janelle and Lloyd are having an affair. Plain as day to everyone but you."

"Now, Wade." Lloyd laughed nervously. "Don't believe an old lady."

"You and I only wanted what was best for the people we love," Ms. Agnes said. "You thought Janelle needed Lloyd's treatments. I thought Sue Ann would be able to walk."

Wade narrowed his eyes as the reality sank in. Slowly, he turned on his heel to face Lloyd. Behind him, the wind howled through the open bay door.

"You run home to Sue Ann," Wade said out of the corner of his mouth.

"What?" Just that quickly, Agnes's face

274

clouded with confusion. "Sue Ann? My baby's home alone." She shuffled toward the door. "Don't worry. Mama's coming home, baby girl."

As Agnes left the building, Lloyd grabbed Kate. "If you shoot me, Wade, the woman dies first. You want that on your conscience?"

Kate's heart skipped wildly.

Lloyd's left arm encircled her neck. The other wrapped tightly around her waist.

"I'll kill you both," Wade sneered.

"You've got it all wrong," the doc whined. His fear-tinged breath soured the air. "Janelle threw herself at me. It wasn't my fault."

Wade cocked the gun.

Heart ready to explode with fright, Kate looked at Heather huddled behind the freezer. The girl tilted her head toward the side exit where the butt of the sheriff's cigarette glowed red against the damp gasoline rag.

A puff of smoke curled into the air.

Lloyd sniffed and spied the problem.

"Turner, you fool. I told you not to smoke in here. You're gonna blow us sky high."

Distracted, Lloyd relaxed his hold on Kate for a split second.

In that instant, she jammed her fist into

his stomach and twisted out of his hold. Just as she did, a shot reverberated through the lab.

Lloyd staggered backward, blood seeping from a bullet wound to his left side.

The sheriff drew his gun and fired at Wade. He dropped to one knee, then collapsed onto the floor.

Nolan grabbed Turner's outstretched arm. The two fought for control of the sheriff's pistol.

"Run, Kate," Nolan screamed. "Save Heather."

Kate took the girl's hand and hobbled to Wade's sedan. Luckily, the keys hung from the ignition. Kate scrambled behind the wheel as Heather jumped in the passenger seat.

"Dad," Heather cried.

Kate glanced up in time to see Nolan and the sheriff on the floor, the gun in Turner's hand.

Near them, the rags burst into flame. A cabinet filled with chemicals hung directly overhead.

Kate twisted the key in the ignition. The engine coughed but didn't catch.

"God, I need help *now*."

Again. This time, the engine purred to a start. Kate jerked the gearshift into Reverse and stepped on the accelerator. The car lunged backward.

Once they cleared the warehouse, Kate shoved the car into Drive.

Rain pounded against the windshield. She turned on the wipers.

Darkness lay ahead. Where were the head-lights?

Kate slapped the steering column, searching for the switch. Nothing.

She groped her hand along the dash. Light switch. Light switch. Where was it?

The car hit a pothole, bounced. Finding a knob, she turned it clockwise and was rewarded with light.

Heather screamed. They were on a collision course with a giant oak.

Kate yanked the wheel. The car skirted the tree.

In the rearview mirror, Kate saw smoke curl out the bay door.

Just like the night at Eddie's cabin. The candle had overturned, and she hadn't reacted.

For the first time, Kate saw everything with a clear eye.

Love is a choice. She heard Nolan's voice play through her mind.

Eddie had chosen not to love her. She hadn't done anything wrong.

Just like her father had chosen not to love her. For whatever reason. She'd never know.

Now, *she* had a choice.

Kate glanced at Heather, sitting ramrod straight in the seat next to her. The girl's eyes were large, her face drawn tight with fear.

Suddenly, Kate knew the truth. She loved Nolan. And loved his daughter like her own.

Kate had to go back. She couldn't let Nolan die because she ran scared again.

As the car shimmied back onto the road, Kate tramped on the brake. The car jerked to a halt.

Heather whipped her head around. "What are you doing?"

"Going back for your father. You take the wheel. Get help, Heather."

"But —"

Kate climbed out of the car and glanced at the open bay door. "You can do it, honey. For your dad."

Heather scooted over to the driver's seat. She gave Kate a quick hug, then slammed the door and stepped on the gas.

Kate watched the car head down the road. With her heart thumping and resolve pushing her forward, Kate staggered back to help the man she loved.

The acrid smell of smoke filled the air as Kate neared the warehouse. She peered through the open bay.

Flames shot upward along the wall, licking the cabinet housing the volatile reagents.

Her heart jerked. Nolan lay facedown on the cold tile floor. Blood pooled around his head.

"Nolan," she screamed, rushing to his side.

Kate gasped as she turned him over. His face was torn and bruised. Blood seeped from his nose and mouth.

"You should see the other guy," a voice behind her said.

Startled, Kate glanced over her shoulder. The sheriff's left eye was swollen shut. His front tooth had been knocked out.

He tottered forward and grabbed Kate's arm, pulling her to her feet. "You caused all this by coming to Mercy."

She tried to wrestle out of his hold. "I didn't do anything except answer a friend's call for help."

Turner tightened his grip, then shuddered as if pain had ripped through his body.

In that instant, Kate drove her shoulder

into his chest.

A rush of air wheezed from his lungs.

She fumbled in her pocket for the syringe. Her fingers slipped over the slick plastic.

Grabbing the shaft, she yanked off the needle's protective sheath.

Whatever medication Edith had selected, let it be fast acting.

Kate jammed the needle into Turner's side and pushed down on the plunger.

"Why you little —"

He grabbed her hair and yanked her head back. His left hand held her like a vise while he raised his right and swung.

She screamed, anticipating the blow.

Before he made contact, his breath hitched.

He released his hold and took two steps backward. Clutching his heart, he collapsed onto the floor.

Kate staggered to Nolan's side.

Flames curled around the reagent cabinet.

Not much time. She grasped Nolan's arms and tugged.

He barely moved an inch. She'd never get Nolan to safety.

The utility cart. Kate hobbled into the surgery room and hurried back, leaning on the cart for support. The wheels clattered over the tile floor.

Pain shot through her leg.

"God, help me," she prayed, finding strength from within.

Clutching Nolan's shoulders, she lifted his heavy torso. Somehow she inched his arms and trunk onto the flat bed of the cart.

Fire crackled behind her. She needed to get Nolan outside and into the clear before the reagents exploded.

"Oh, God, save this man," she prayed, pushing the cart toward the open bay door.

Her leg gave out. She fell. Her knee screamed in protest. Kate forced herself up and shoved forward, ignoring the pain, thinking only of Nolan.

Outside the wind howled, and rain splattered the water-soaked earth.

Kate struggled to remain upright, pushing, finally gaining momentum as the cart broke into the stormy night.

She had to get Nolan across the driveway and clear of the building.

Giant oaks lined the road. The cart hit an exposed root and tipped.

"Nolan!" His lifeless body slid onto the wet ground.

Kate reached for his wrist. Searching for his pulse, she felt nothing.

The wind swirled around them. Her hair blew into her eyes. Fat drops of rain fell against her face.

"Oh, God, don't let him die."

"God won't help you, Kate."

She jerked around at the voice, barely audible above the howling wind.

Lloyd Samuels stood a few feet away. A gun dangled from the fingers of his right hand. His left arm hung limp at his side.

Blood matted his shirt where the bullet had pierced his flesh. He staggered toward her.

Black smoke wafted from the interior of the lab and disappeared into the night.

"Don't you understand, Kate? I have to win. My work's too important."

"Since when is killing people important?" she screamed above the roar of the storm. She inched her body over Nolan's. She had to protect the man she loved.

"*Do no harm,* Lloyd. Remember the reason you went into medicine?"

"Money. Fame. Power. That's what I want, Kate. And I'll have it once you and Nolan are dead. Then, I'll be able to finish my regeneration research."

Kate shook her head. "You'll never find peace, Lloyd. You're filled with hate."

The doc laughed and took a step forward. "Looks like Nolan's dead already. Funny, your God didn't save him. Explain that."

"I can't. But he's a loving God, and I trust He knows what's best."

"Then you're a fool."

Wind raged. Trees bent toward the rain-soaked ground.

Lloyd aimed the gun at Kate.

A sense of peace spread over her. She wrapped her arm around Nolan and, feeling no fear, looked defiantly at the man who planned to take her life.

A deafening roar filled the air as the corner of the clinic exploded. A portion of the roof tore free and sailed through the night.

Seeing the flying debris, Lloyd dropped his gun and ran for cover in the cluster of oaks.

Sirens howled in the distance. Help was coming, but not in time for Nolan. Not in time for her.

A second explosion shredded the corner of the building.

Kate pictured the painting in Nolan's office. She saw the rays of light break through the storm clouds and felt the warm flow of unconditional love pour down upon her.

"I love you, Nolan," Kate whispered.

She held him tightly as shrapnel rained down around them.

TWENTY-ONE

Kate opened her eyes. Sunlight streamed through the window. Where was she?

An IV bag hung at the side of her bed and dripped fluid along the tubing into her left arm.

Suddenly, she remembered. The storm, the explosion —

Nolan!

She blinked back tears, but they spilled over her bottom lashes and ran down her cheeks.

She hadn't been able to save him. A crushing sense of loss settled over her.

The door pushed open. Someone stepped into the room.

"Kate?"

She turned at the voice. "Heather!"

The girl ran to her bedside and clutched Kate's outstretched hand. "We were so worried about you. The doctor wasn't sure —"

Kate rubbed Heather's arm. "Oh, honey,

I'm so sorry about your dad."

She looked confused. "But, Kate —"

The door opened again. A nurse peered into the room. "Feel like a little company, Ms. Murphy?"

Kate shook her head. "No. Not now. Ask them to come back later."

"I knew you were too stubborn for your own good," a voice bellowed from the hallway.

Kate couldn't believe her ears.

She glanced up at Heather, who was smiling from ear to ear. "The doctor said Dad could leave his room for a few minutes."

Kate struggled to sit up. Pain cut through her left leg. She managed to raise her head as the nurse guided a wheelchair through the doorway.

Nolan's arm hung in a sling, his head was bandaged and a patch covered his right eye, but he was alive.

The nurse pushed him to Kate's bedside. "I'll give you a few minutes alone."

"I thought —" Kate shook her head as if to ensure she wasn't dreaming. "I thought you had died."

"The EMTs thought we both had. Don't know if you remember, but a vinyl bay door landed on us. The sheriff over in Summerton's convinced that's what saved us from the flying debris."

"Tell her about Jimmy," Heather enthused.

Nolan smiled up at his daughter. "Heather drove to the cabin. A couple of the kids from school were there. Luckily, they had a cell phone. Heather called Jimmy, and he alerted his brother, Miguel, at the fire department."

"What about the others?" Kate asked.

"They found Lloyd trapped under a fallen tree. Must have killed him instantly. The sheriff's dead, as well."

Kate gasped. "I injected him with the syringe Edith had filled."

"Probably why he had meperidine something-or-other in his blood."

"Meperidine hydrochloride? That's another name for Demerol. But that shouldn't have killed him."

"It didn't. He died from a massive heart attack. Edith was a bit luckier. She's being held in the Summerton jail, awaiting trial."

"Edith survived the explosion?"

"Amazingly, yes. So did Wade. His wound was serious but not life threatening. He's got a good Atlanta lawyer. Claims he and Janelle were brainwashed by the doc." Nolan shrugged. "I'm sure the truth will come out in court."

"Dad has to testify in California," Heather said. "When he does, can I stay with you in Atlanta?"

Kate smiled. "Of course you can." She glanced at Nolan. "The transplant tourist racket?"

"The Beverly Hills Specialty Center has closed permanently. Your boss provided information about medical records the center falsified."

"That must have been what Dr. Elders talked to Jason about."

"It was. The authorities also uncovered incriminating evidence of wrongdoing from a woman who had planned to buy an organ in India. Thank goodness, she had second thoughts and canceled her trip."

"The governor wants to give Dad an award," Heather added with pride. "A story in the L.A. papers said he acted heroically."

Kate smiled. "That's one story the papers got right."

For the first time, Kate saw Nolan blush.

Someone knocked, then pushed open the door. Miguel peeked inside. "Tracy and I wanted to stop by for a minute."

He eased Tracy forward in a wheelchair, a small bundle in her arms.

"So I could show off my little darling," Tracy said. She pulled down the edge of the blanket. "Kate, meet my daughter."

Miguel squeezed Tracy's hand. "She's my baby girl, too."

Tracy beamed. "Well, of course, honey. You had an important part in all this."

The baby's eyes opened.

Kate sighed. "She's beautiful."

"Tina Espinosa kept telling me everything with Miguel would work out." Tracy smiled down at her baby. "That's why we named our little girl Tina."

A lump formed in Kate's throat and tears of joy filled her eyes.

"Have you heard about the wedding?" Tracy asked.

"Wedding?" Kate and Nolan both said in unison.

"Miguel asked me to marry him." Tracy's eyes sparkled with joy. "Everyone's invited."

Nolan raised his hand. "Kate's going to need surgery on her leg and extensive rehabilitation." He glanced at Kate. "Seems you completely ruptured your ACL while you were trying to save my life."

"We'll work around her rehab schedule," Tracy assured them. "Anyway, Sue Ann wants all of us — Miguel, Jimmy, Tina and me — to move in with her. She needs help, and she's got the big house she wants to keep."

"How is Sue Ann?" Kate asked.

"She's okay now the medicine Lloyd was giving her finally worked its way out of her system. Sue Ann had overheard the doc tell Edith how he lied to Ms. Agnes so she would fund his research. When Sue Ann confronted Lloyd, he upped her medicine to keep her quiet."

"And what about Aggie?"

"She's under psychiatric care at the state institution over in Harding. They don't think she'll ever have to stand trial."

"Dementia compounded the problem," Miguel added before he turned to Nolan. "Hank said to thank you for putting in a good word for him at the garage. He's been promoted to assistant manager."

"Happy to help out," Nolan said with a smile.

Tracy glanced at the clock on the wall. "Time to get going before this little one needs to eat again." She grabbed Heather's hand. "Jimmy said he'll pick you up in front of the hospital."

The teen turned to her father and dropped a kiss on his cheek. "Thanks for letting me go to the movies with Jimmy and the other kids." Heather brushed her lips against Kate's forehead before she dashed from the room. Tracy and Miguel waved as they followed her out.

Once they were alone, Kate rubbed her fingers over Nolan's bruised right hand. "I prayed so hard for you. This time, God heard my prayer."

He edged closer. "Kate, I believe God wants us to be together."

She swallowed. "Together?"

He took her hand in his. "Heather needs a mother. I need a wife." He let out an exasperated breath and shook his head. "I always get tongue-tied around you. Let me try again."

Her heart pounded in her chest.

"Kate Murphy, I love you. You're beautiful and intelligent and gutsy, and I've never met a woman who made me act like such a fool."

She laughed. "Is that a good thing?"

"It's a very good thing." He rubbed his fingers down her cheek. "After your surgery, I want you to complete your Ph.D. so I can call you Dr. Murphy."

She raised her eyebrows in anticipation.

"And then, I thought we'd take some time to get to know each other better before . . ." Nolan cleared his throat. "Before I ask you to marry me."

A warm glow spread over Kate. Her heart filled with love. Unconditional love for

Nolan, for Heather and for God, who loved her beyond all understanding.

Kate didn't say anything. She couldn't. Nolan had lowered his mouth to hers. His kiss was the sweetest she'd ever known.

EPILOGUE

Kate took her seat on the raised platform and smiled at Nolan, sitting in the front row of the crowd of people who had gathered on the lawn. She rubbed the engagement ring on her left hand and winked at Heather, sitting between Nolan and Jimmy.

Ten days from now, Kate would become Mrs. Nolan Price. She nearly laughed out loud with joy.

Sitting in a wheelchair next to Kate, Sue Ann whispered, "Bet I know what you're thinking about."

Kate smiled. "I'm blessed, Sue Ann."

The woman nodded. "Aren't we all."

Jason Bannister moved to the podium. Tall and distinguished with a wisp of gray at his temples, he smiled at Kate before he spoke.

"Ladies and gentlemen, it is indeed an honor for me to open the Heartwell Research Laboratory, a division of Bannister Scientific, here in Mercy, Georgia. Bannister

Scientific is dedicated to making this world a better and safer place through the advancement of science. The Heartwell facility will expand our capabilities, and under the able leadership of its clinical director, I know mankind will reap the benefits."

He paused for a moment and pointed to Sue Ann. "I'd be remiss if I didn't thank Ms. Heartwell for her vision and the gift of this laboratory."

Kate reached over and clutched Sue Ann's hand as the audience applauded.

"And now, ladies and gentlemen," Jason continued, "I'd like to present the clinical director of Heartwell Research Laboratory, Dr. Kate Murphy."

The crowd rose to their feet, cheering loudly. No one was as enthusiastic as Nolan. Kate smiled, hearing his voice boom over all the others.

As the crowd settled back into their chairs, Kate glanced over her shoulder at the gleaming new facility. Sue Ann had wanted the laboratory built on the site of the aluminum structure that had been destroyed.

"So something good could come from all the pain," she had told Kate.

In front of the lab's glass entrance, a large bronze fountain in the shape of a heart sprayed life-giving water into a brick pool. Daylilies waved their blooms over rows of red begonias and purple periwinkles.

Kate turned back to the audience and stepped to the microphone. Tracy waved at Kate while her baby girl cooed in Miguel's arms. Pauline and Hank sat nearby, their first child due any day.

She was blessed by the people of Mercy, but most of all God had been Kate's refuge in the storm. She knew now without a shadow of doubt that He would walk with her into the tomorrows of her life, protecting her, loving her, blessing her.

Kate had so much for which to be thankful — a wonderful man who loved her dearly, a beautiful daughter to call her own and a lifetime of love that would stretch into eternity.

"Ladies and gentlemen, friends, neighbors, I'd like to give thanks for all that has happened to bring us to this point. And most especially, I'd like to thank our loving God in whom all things are possible."

Dear Reader,

Kate Murphy never expects a quick trip to Mercy, Georgia, will change her life forever. Abandoned as a child by her father, Kate feels unworthy of God's love. When her life is threatened and it appears everything she holds dear will be taken from her, she is finally able to turn to God.

Widowed for eight months, Nolan is close to unraveling the mystery surrounding his wife's untimely death when Kate crashes into his life. Kate soon discovers Nolan's overprotective nature is threatening to destroy his fragile relationship with his daughter. With Kate's help, Nolan learns love sometimes requires letting go, and Kate realizes she doesn't have to earn God's love, or Nolan's. Both are freely given.

Just as in this story, God often reveals Himself in unexpected ways. I hope you will be open to His presence in your life and allow Him to fill you with His mercy and love.

Thank you for reading *Scared to Death*. Visit me online at www.debbygiusti.com and write to me at debby@debbygiusti .com.

Wishing you abundant blessings,
Debby Giusti

QUESTIONS FOR DISCUSSION

1. Tina's phone call and journal entries reveal her desire to reconcile with Kate. Why did they remain estranged for so long? Are there relationships in your life that need reconciliation?

2. Kate feels responsible for her father's abandonment. How does that affect her relationship with others? Do you carry any pain from your past? How can faith in an all-loving God help you to heal?

3. To Kate, the gold cross symbolizes faith in a God she has shut out of her life. How does her life change once the cross is returned to her?

4. Kate tells Nolan that communication is key in dealing with his daughter. When does his relationship with Heather begin to improve? Do you think communication

is important in all relationships? Why?

5. Nolan tells Kate that human love is a choice. Do you agree? Why or why not?

6. Overprotective of his teenage daughter, Nolan learns love sometimes requires letting go. Have there been times in your life when you've had to "let go" of someone you loved? What happened?

7. Explain what Nolan means when he wishes he could be a Simon of Cyrene for his daughter. Have there been people who have helped carry your cross in tough times?

8. How is Nolan's relationship with the Lord revealed throughout the story? Do you feel that he is striving to lead a good Christian life despite the mistakes he makes with his daughter?

9. Dr. Lloyd Samuels has a twisted sense of right and wrong and believes the end justifies the means. Do you think that's ever true? How does your faith help you ensure your values are never compromised?

10. Sue Ann wanted the Heartwell Research

Laboratory built on the site where the aluminum warehouse had formerly stood so something good could come from all the pain. Have there been times when you've invited God into the midst of your pain? What happened when you did?

ABOUT THE AUTHOR

Debby Giusti is a medical technologist who loves working with test tubes and petri dishes almost as much as she loves to write. Growing up as an army brat, Debby met and married her husband — then a captain in the army — at Fort Knox, Kentucky. Together they traveled throughout the world, raised three wonderful army brats of their own and now see the military tradition carried on in their son who's also in the army. She was always busy with church, school and community activities, so when Debby and her family moved to Atlanta, Georgia, she knew it was time to settle down and write her first book. Despite occasional moments of wanderlust, Debby spends most of her time writing inspirational romantic suspense for Steeple Hill Books.

Debby wants to hear from her readers. Contact her c/o Steeple Hill Books, 233

Broadway, New York, NY 10279. Visit her Web site at www.debbygiusti.com and e-mail her at debby@debbygiusti.com.

The employees of Thorndike Press hope you have enjoyed this Large Print book. All our Thorndike and Wheeler Large Print titles are designed for easy reading, and all our books are made to last. Other Thorndike Press Large Print books are available at your library, through selected bookstores, or directly from us.

For information about titles, please call:
    (800) 223-1244

or visit our Web site at:
    http://gale.cengage.com/thorndike

To share your comments, please write:
    Publisher
    Thorndike Press
    295 Kennedy Memorial Drive
    Waterville, ME 04901